total eclipse of the witches

Lauren Vinn

To Grandad Lenny,

You took a walk through a sunset
And since that day we knew
When the dark night brings us the stars
The brightest one is you.

I hope we're making you proud.

Brannon

I had hoped for something extraordinary…

Asher

I'd never say it out loud, but I've never felt more unsatisfied in my life. It's not Brannon. She's still everything. That's never changed. What I'm unsatisfied with is my understanding of the supernatural world.

I thought I understood the Myst. And the pendants, and my role in this. But it's quickly become apparent that I don't. Now I have more questions than answers. I want to know about the Sol and the Lunar witches. I want to know why I never knew about them before. But most of all, I need to know who left those words, back in Heston last year, in the midst of Brannon's quest.

If only you knew...it started with me.

What does it even mean? What started and with who?

The frustration I felt was overwhelming. I wanted so badly to know their name, or their face or anything. But I had nowhere to begin. Nothing even close to a starting point. All I had were scraps of paper with confusing words handwritten on them. This person didn't want to reveal their self. At least not easily. They wanted to help, for some unknown reason, in rehoming the power of the Myst. And if they wanted to get into our heads, then they'd done a very good job of it.

Brannon

I have powers. It still doesn't sound possible, but it is. And I do.

It's not what I expected. But then again, I didn't know what to expect. I don't have a wand and magic doesn't shoot out of my fingertips. Juno said that the magic would get to know us before granting us power, and I think that's what happened.

I wouldn't call myself a witch. I can't create spells or chant in Latin like Juno does. The magic from the Myst granted me the ability to read people's emotions. I can feel anger from a mile off, and I've learnt that happiness really is contagious. Faking a mood around me doesn't work, because I can tell. This also means that I can cheer someone up who's pretending to be happy, because I can feel their sadness.

It's not the type of magic that a witch would have. It's harmless. It's safe. It's Amory friendly.

As for Asher and me, I love him more than ever. And I know he loves me more than ever, too. But due to my new ability to read his feelings, I also know that he hasn't been the same since it all happened. I know that, just like me, he feels unsatisfied. He needs to know the identity of the mysterious helper.

Asher

It's not like I had to declare my desire for answers out loud. Brannon knew. She knew everything that I felt.

She always had been an emotional person. Always invested in my feelings, and always deeply caught up in her own. Her anger led to outbursts, her sadness to isolation and her love led her to me.

As for my power, it got to know me just as well. I have always hated the unknown. Uncertainty is something I struggle with. Waiting for Brannon to make her decision about the pendants was one of the hardest days of my life. My anxiety was uncontrollable. I wished for the ability to see into the future. It's later than I would have hoped, but it's true that if you wish for something hard enough, it will come true. Because now I can do exactly that.

I can't tell the future of anyone's entire life. My powers only allow me to see a few minutes ahead of everyone else, which is more useful than I first thought.

For example, Brannon and I went for a walk a few weeks ago. My mind forced me to see an old lady tripping over a branch in the forest and being seriously hurt. We rushed to the location, removed the branch and waited for the woman to pass. When she did, there was nothing in her way to trip her up.

The other day when we were at the beach, a young boy was swimming further away from the shore than he should have been. I knew that a series of strong waves were approaching, so I convinced a lifeguard to jet ski out to him. He wouldn't have been strong enough to swim through the wave. It would have swallowed him whole. In moments like that, my power is the best thing about me.

But that's not why I love the powers that Brannon and I have. I love them because they're not too much. We aren't a threat to humanity. We can still live a normal life as normal people. And despite the fact that she can read emotions, I can see the future and we anchor a supernatural afterlife, we are exactly that. Normal.

Brannon

It's been eight months since my supernatural treasure hunt around Heston. It's nearing the end of May and the sun is getting hotter as each day passes.

Mum and Marley joined us for Christmas. They stayed in my cabin with me. It was perfect. Marley found it fascinating that I had my own house. Or shed, as he called it. Mum thought it was beautiful and was shocked to know that Asher's dad built it for me free of charge. They had welcomed me into their family like I was one of their own and, finally, she was able to see that.

They loved it here and it made Mum happy knowing that I was living in such an amazing place. Asher would take Marley paddle boarding at sunset whilst me and Mum helped Tammy, Asher's mum, prepare dinner. Roger filtered the discussions about magic whilst they were with us because they didn't need to hear it. I don't want them involved. When they said goodbye, there were no sad tears because everyone was happy. And as much as I missed them, everyone was exactly where they were meant to be.

Me and Asher seemed fine, but I was scared that, as the months went on, we wouldn't find each other as exciting. That we'd, perhaps, get sick of each other and spend less time together. But that never happened.

I wait for him to show up at my door every morning, smiling his beautiful smile. I feel excited whenever I see him, like it's the first time all over again. I get butterflies when he kisses me, and I still feel like the luckiest person alive. And most of all, he's still my best friend. The only person who makes me laugh uncontrollably and love unconditionally.

Our life together couldn't be better. It's been that way since the first day I saw him. However, he was struggling with adapting to this new life of ours.

It was the headaches.

Asher

I hadn't felt pain quite like it until my first episode. I passed into the Myst like normal, and then the pain started. Like a stab to the skull. Over and over again. It was the first time that I couldn't give someone a peaceful goodbye because I could barely open my eyes or talk from the pain. And it didn't stop when I woke up. The shooting pains continued for at least another hour. I didn't think it was right. I thought something had gone wrong, until Brannon said that it's perfectly normal and that I'd be fine.

The fact that she had been going through that pain her whole life, that she chose to keep going through it for me, meant I admired her more than ever and loved her more than that.

Brannon hated seeing me in pain, especially because she knew exactly how it felt. But I think it's made it easier for her to accept herself as an Amory now that she isn't the only one being punished.

I've been experiencing headaches for months; I'm getting used to them. The pain isn't a shock anymore and the headache tablets that Brannon has make it bearable. Now that summer is on its way, making plans with Brannon is the only thing on my mind.

I want to do everything with her. I want to have barbecues on the beach and swim in the sea until the sun melts away. I want to mess around in the lakes and stargaze with her under the moon. I want to watch her skin bronze and her silver hair lighten to a lilac colour. I want this summer to be just as good as the last, hopefully better.

I want to forget about the words and the stranger. And I want her to forget as well.

Brannon

"What do you want to do today then?" Asher called through the door as I stepped out of the shower.

"It's warm today. Shall we go to the beach?" I asked.

"Sounds good."

I'm always at my happiest when we're at the beach. The holidays haven't started yet either, which means it won't be packed with people.

We don't get to go every day. Even if we did, I wouldn't get sick of it, but Asher and I haven't been for a while. We've been occupied, studying anything and everything we could find about the Myst and Juno and the witches. It was the first time I'd enjoyed studying. Every account of the Myst was different, which made for interesting reading, even though I knew that most of them were lies. We both moved on from studying the Myst pretty quickly because we were interested in something else. The Lunar witches. We hadn't found any answers. If Juno hadn't mentioned them, we'd have no idea of their existence.

I suggested the beach because it would allow us to escape the books and have a day together. After all, it was only ourselves that were forcing us to study.

I walked out of the bathroom with my hair pinned up by a hair claw. Asher was laying on my bed, arms behind his head, staring at me.

"I know, not my best look," I said.

He laughed softly. "I don't think you could look bad if you tried."

Butterflies fluttered happily around my stomach. He still has that power over me.

I changed into a swimming costume and some shorts, Asher staring at me all the while. I knew how much admiration he felt towards me. But even if I couldn't read his emotions, his eyes said it all. We grabbed some towels and headed to the beach.

Asher

The sand felt hot beneath my feet. A feeling I'd been missing. The waves overlapped each other elegantly and the sun glistened on the ocean's surface. A feeling of nostalgia hit me as I reminisced about last summer and how it felt during summer camp.

"I miss it, too," Brannon said.

I smiled at her and then laid our towels on sunbeds. "I'll be back in a minute. Going to get us some drinks," I said.

I came back with pink lemonade, her favourite. She was laying on her sunbed, rubbing sun cream into her silky skin. I still find it hard to believe that she's my girlfriend.

She thanked me as I placed it on the small table between the beds.

The sound of the sea and the heat from the sun melted almost all of my problems away. But there was still one thought lingering in my mind that wouldn't leave until I confronted it.

Life didn't feel settled. When Brannon kept her pendant, I naively believed that we'd have a peaceful life moving forward. I thought that stress would be a feeling of the past. But since my family got ill and Brannon had to return to Heston and then we got given powers, all I have done is worried. Because I don't feel like that's the last of it.

I was stupid to believe that, after four hundred years of waiting, our lives would be normal with the pendants. No matter how loved Brannon makes me feel, and she really does, I am always waiting for something to happen. Something to ruin what we have. Worrying that I might not be able to protect her from the supernatural world like her dad did.

Brannon

I was wrong in thinking that the beach would be an escape from all supernatural things. Asher's mind was restless. He felt anxious, stressed, worried. Scared.

I didn't bring it up. I waited for him to talk to me. He didn't like it when I read his emotions. I guess it invaded his privacy and I wouldn't like it either.

"Brannon?"

I turned to face him. I could tell this wasn't going to be a light conversation.

"Asher?"

"Are you satisfied with our life?" he asked.

I didn't answer immediately. The intriguing thing was, I wasn't sure at first. I have nothing to complain about when it comes to Asher. So technically, our life together satisfied me very well. I pondered on it, before replying, "Yes."

He looked confused. He didn't believe me, so I explained myself. "Asher, our life together is more than I could ask for. You're the best thing to ever happen to me. No one has ever loved me like you love me. Of course I'm satisfied with our life." He listened to me, invested in my every word. "But if you asked me if I'm satisfied with my own life, I would say no."

"Why not?"

"I never will be until I know who that stranger is."

He sighed and dropped his head to his chest. "I don't know how to fix that for you," he said, disappointed in himself.

I didn't want him to feel like this. It wasn't his fault. "Are you satisfied with your life?" I asked him.

He thought about it for a moment, probably realising that there was no point in pretending. I'd know anyway.

"No, not really. I want to know who it was too," he admitted.

"Exactly, and there's nothing I can do to fix that for you. So, I guess we will just have to move on," I said, unable to accept my own words but hoping that he would.

We didn't talk for the next few minutes. Asher was lost in his thoughts. We knew that the person who had secretly helped me in Heston had more knowledge of the supernatural world than we did. They had known what objects I needed and must have been close to me to know when I needed them. It was a discomforting feeling. Especially knowing that they had left their message, those mysterious words, purposely trying to get into our heads. It had worked brilliantly. The only problem is that we never knew, and likely never will know, who they are. I also don't know what else to suggest to Asher other than to just move on, even though I can't do that myself.

"Maybe you're right," he said. "Maybe we need to move on. I mean, properly move on. Stop studying books all day trying to find answers that are probably not even written down. We need to start living again."

"I agree."

"We live in the most beautiful place in the world. And summer is nearly here," he continued, "We've spent months inside. Sure, we're more than happy inside together, but I think we could be happier out here."

"We could be," I said, nodding a little hesitantly.

"Well, you aren't really saying much, Bran."

"I'm just letting you talk, Ash. Everything you're saying is right. I want to have fun and forget about everything else. But I don't think you will be able to."

He was used to my honesty, but it still took him by surprise sometimes.

"Okay. Maybe you're right. But how about we try to enjoy summer, and we will continue our hunt for answers after?" he suggested.

I smiled, knowing this was more realistic and a plan that I could get on board with. The best option wasn't to avoid it, but perhaps postponing it was all we could do.

"There's that smile that I love," he said, sitting up and reaching for my hands to sit me up opposite him.

"I think that's a much better idea than pretending we can click our fingers and forget it," I said. "So, where do we start then?"

Without warning, he picked me up and slung me over his shoulder. He ran through the sand, fighting the ground as he sunk into it. I felt the muscles in his shoulders as I clung on to him, knowing that he wouldn't drop me. His feet met the water, and I could feel droplets of the sea splashing in my face. He kept running until he was waist-deep in the blue water, a froth of white bubbles forming and breaking against him. Then he lowered me into the sea, until my feet touched the ground. He took my face in the palms of his hands and kissed me.

"We start here."

Asher

She spent the next few hours floating in my arms. We only got out of the sea to eat lunch. Later, we sat on paddle boards, drifting in a light breeze to the accompanying lap of soft waves, the scent of the ocean all around as we sipped lemonade, watching the sky transform from blue to gold as the sun set behind the horizon. She was my happiness and most definitely my escape. It doesn't matter what we do this summer. All I want is to see her happy.

We spent the night talking in bed, about how we felt when we first met and how she never thought her life would pan out this way but how she's so happy that it did. It felt like a break from the heavy seriousness that our lives had adopted.

Brannon wanted to make ice pops the next day. We picked different flavoured juice from the shop and mixed it with water to freeze overnight. Then we spent the evening in the garden with my family.

The day after that we walked for hours. We trekked up the mountains, tan lines forming around the straps on Brannon's shoulders. The first time we did this walk we kept a secret from each other. Ironically, it was the same secret. Now there is no one in the world who knows me better.

When we got home, we enjoyed Brannon's ice pops and reflected on another amazing day together. Summer is the best time to make memories, and we were doing just that.

The thought of the stranger still crossed my mind, but not enough to ruin my day anymore. I think that was the case for Brannon, too. She had been concentrating on research and finding answers recently. A side to her that showed determination and persistence and intelligence. The past few days, she had been fun and adventurous and full of life. I loved every side of her, but this was my favourite.

Brannon

In a matter of days, our stressful life became a life full of adventure. One of the reasons I love him so much is that he makes everything better, and he's always up for anything. My hopes for summer were growing.

We decided to meet up with Asher's friends in the evening. They had welcomed me into their friendship group and treated me as if I'd been there from the start. Unfortunately, there were no other girls in the group, but my best friend of my entire life is a boy, Blain, so I didn't mind.

The boys threw a frisbee across the beach whilst I sat and read a book. Every so often I looked up into the sky and found a spectrum of colours, fresh from a paint palette. I could hear the slight breeze meeting the surface of the water. As I watched the few clouds drift by, time stopped. The sudden urge to fade away into the glorious view flooded my body. I didn't want to stop looking. I knew, the first time I saw it, that I'd never be able to take this view for granted. I loved it. I loved watching the sun set.

Asher was running towards me, his toned figure sweating under his open shirt and his tight ringlets falling on his forehead. He leant down to pick up his drink and kiss my cheek before sitting beside me on a sunbed.

"Wow. That's a beautiful sunset," he said, staring at it with admiration.

I loved seeing him like this. Happy and free from his thoughts.

His friends, Dan and Scotty, came over to have a drink too.

"Dan, can you do me a favour," Asher asked, handing Dan his phone. "Take a picture of us, please."

"Sure thing," Dan said.

Asher took my hand and walked me closer to the water. We faced Dan, arms around each other. The wind blew my dress up slightly and Asher noticed me rushing to hold it down. He moved to the other side of me, blocking the wind.

"I can't take the picture if you keep moving, guys," Dan said.

"He's trying to find his best side," Scotty joked.

"What's your best side, Asher?" Dan asked.

Asher gave a soft laugh, as if the answer should be obvious. "She is my best side."

He looked down at me and smiled, placing his lips gently on my head. Dan captured it. Then we smiled, and he captured that too.

Words couldn't describe the way I felt in that moment.

We took the phone from Dan and looked through the photos.

Asher

I was standing in black shorts, my white shirt unbuttoned. Then there was Brannon. Her strappy white dress and purple hair waving behind her back. Her décolletage glistening, her eyes full of happiness. And the most beautiful sky in the background. This. This is everything.

The next morning, Brannon walked to my house to have breakfast with my parents. It was the first time this year that dad had to put the ceiling fans on because it was a hot morning. Mum made a fruit salad and laid chocolate filled croissants on the table.

Brannon stood at the door, jawline exposed because her hair was pulled back in a ponytail.

"Good morning," I said, kissing her on the cheek.

She smiled, brightening my day before it had even begun.

"Wow, breakfast looks great," Brannon said, walking into the kitchen.

She said hello to my parents before we filled bowls up with juicy strawberries and slices of mango and pineapple.

"What did you two get up to yesterday, then?" mum asked as we were sitting in the garden eating.

"We met up with Dan and Scotty. Got the frisbee out on the beach," I said.

"Sounds lovely. Brannon if you ever wanted to invite any of your friends to camp, I'm sure Roger can arrange something."

Brannon smiled, not knowing what to say. She'd love, more than anything, to invite Blain here again. But he always says no.

"Thank you. I'll bare that in mind," Brannon said.

Brannon

I missed Blain so much. I thought we would've seen each other by now but I know how long grief can last and I didn't want to pressure him into seeing me if he wasn't ready.

After breakfast, Asher and I decided to explore a new part of camp. Roger had installed a natural swimming pool next to the sea. The sea water spilled over the edge, filling it up. He also had a waterfall built. The turquoise water ran down one of the cliff sides, falling into the newly structured pool.

We climbed the steps to the top of the pool, which was above ground level. When the tide came in at night, it splashed against the side of the pool and cascaded over the edges. The surface wasn't smooth, so we brought towels and pillows to sit on.

"Dad's outdone himself this time," Asher said, looking at the bright cyan blue sky. Not a cloud was in sight and the sun cast a blinding yellow shine over the clear azure sea.

"It's beautiful," I said, truly amazed by how natural a manmade pool could look.

"Let's get in," Asher said.

He took off his T-shirt and I removed my dress so that we were in our swimwear.

I sat on the edge, dipping my legs in first. The water was warm and enticing. I watched as Asher lowered his body in, letting himself sink right down until his hair was underwater. Soon enough, his head popped back up and he was telling me how salty it tasted and not to open my eyes when I went under as it would sting.

Sometimes I wish it was the other way around, and he could see how I feel. How I love him like the moon loves the sun.

"I'm thinking of inviting Blain up here again," I said.

Asher swum over and rested his arms on my knees.

"That's fine, you know he's always welcome. But what if he says no?" he asked.

The thought of it made me sad. Blain was like my twin. I needed him.

"Well, I'll be sad. But I'm going to keep asking him because he's my best friend."

"Okay, let's send him a message then. Fingers crossed he comes this time," he said, taking my hand and kissing it.

I slid in, the warmth of the water surrounding me. We swam to the edge of the pool, looking into the distance.

Satisfied.

Asher

Dad had discussed with me that the camp, one day, would be mine. He told me that I needed to start working, learning the roles of a manager. Seeing his recent creation increased the pressure I already felt. The Curators who owned the camp before him hadn't made this many incredible changes and I wanted to continue to do his work in updating things. Knowing the happiness it brought me and Brannon, it was important to ensure that I could offer the same thing to other people.

We got back to Brannon's cabin before the pitch-black darkness of the night arrived.

"When are you going to message Blain, then?" I asked.

She had just turned the hob off and the smell of smoky fajitas filled my nostrils.

"I'll do it now. He might reply before we go to bed."

She sat beside me so that I could see her typing. I noticed several messages before, of Brannon checking in with Blain and asking him how he is. All of them had been ignored, and I felt a subtle surge of anger towards him. Losing someone is hard, but it wasn't Brannon's fault. She was trying her best to be there for him, and he wasn't even giving her the chance. It may be insensitive of me, but I felt like she deserved better.

The message she sent read, *'Hello. How are you? I really miss you and would love it if you'd let Asher's dad fly you out to camp. Spending a couple of weeks here could really help you. Please think about it. All my love, as always.'*

She looked at me with a smile.

"Fingers crossed," she said.

We often competed over who could cook the best fajitas but as we sat there eating the dinner she had just made, it was clear she had won. We laughed as I surrendered to her victory. Her smug face was cute. She knew she would win eventually.

We were drying up the plates when her phone pinged. I assumed it was her mum or Marley messaging her. I was pleasantly surprised to find out I was wrong.

"It's Blain," she announced.

I was shocked. "That was quick. What did he say?"

Brannon passed me her phone.

'Hey, B! That would be lovely, thank you so much for the invite. One thing though, do you think it would be okay if I brought my nan? I don't want to leave her alone whilst she is going through this.'

Although his response was what Brannon had been hoping for, I felt concerned. His attitude had completely shifted from being so closed off to being the bubbly Blain that I had first met. Whilst I felt happy for Brannon, I couldn't help but feel like something was off.

Brannon

Asher wasn't convinced that Blain was being genuine. I could feel it. I understood why, but I didn't care to entertain it. Blain had finally shown glimpses of his old self and was ready to spend time with me again. I felt an abundance of relief that we were still, after this time, best friends.

"What do you think? Can his nan join him here?" I asked Asher.

"I'll call dad and let you know."

I felt an excitement bubble in the pit of my stomach. I started to think of all the things Blain and I could do together. Days on the beach. Relaxing at the spa. Bonfires. Crashing camp parties.

I'd get to show him my new life. My cabin. The duties I'd given myself around camp. The staff who were now friends. This happy, content side to me that had only flourished since living here.

I'd get to cheer him up and help him find his own happiness again. I could talk to his nan who I hadn't seen since moving to camp.

This could be just what the both of us need to move forward in life. Blain coming here could fix everything.

Asher walked back into the kitchen, a false smile on his face.

"Dad said that his nan coming will be fine. He is going to arrange their flights and transport tomorrow, as well as allocating a cabin for them to stay in."

"I can't believe it, thank you so much!"

"He's only going to book one-way tickets. He said we can arrange their return when they're here. Is that okay?" Asher asked.

"Yes, that's brilliant. I'll let Blain know. Thank you!"

I messaged Blain the information straight away and by the following morning, Roger had booked their flights and a cabin was being prepped for their stay.

Asher

I didn't tell Brannon about my concerns. Aside from the fact that she probably already knew how I felt, I didn't feel it necessary to ruin her happiness and excitement. Blain would be arriving at camp later this evening.

I felt like it was a suspiciously quick turnaround, but I guess it isn't like he or his nan had to cancel plans. Blain doesn't have an education or a career to think of right now and his nan is retired. It's easy for them to jump on a plane to Greece. But that wasn't where my concerns stemmed from.

A few days ago, he had ignored Brannon's messages about his wellbeing, and it didn't seem like he had any intention of reigniting their friendship. Now he has instantly agreed to come and see her in another country. It was almost as if someone had permitted him to be his old self again and that he could now press the play button on their lifelong friendship that he hadn't entertained for months.

It was hard, but I tried not to think too far into it. All would become clear when Blain arrived, and I would be able to tell his true intentions from a face-to-face interaction.

Brannon spent the morning and early afternoon baking sweet treats to leave in their cabin for their arrival.

"Blain loves these brownies. It's Aunt Pat's secret recipe," Brannon excitedly informed me.

I was happy she was happy. That's all that matters right now.

Brannon wanted to take a tray of these infamous brownies to my house as a gift to my parents for arranging and allowing Blain's stay. After this, we headed on a walk around camp to make sure the grounds were clear of litter before the evening coach load of holiday guests arrived.

"So, I guess I'm going to lose you to Blain for the next couple of weeks," I said.

She giggled in her adorable way. "Maybe."

She picked up an abandoned bottle and placed it in the bin before continuing to talk.

"I've missed him so much. It's been really hard to go from talking to someone every day and always having their name pop up on your phone to not talking at all," she explained.

"Do you not feel angry that he hasn't spoken to you for so long?" I asked.

"How can I be? He lost his grandad. I've been sad without him, but I understand that grief takes time. I couldn't expect him to be himself after everything he was going through."

I've never met someone as compassionate and caring as Brannon. Her heart is even more beautiful than her face. No matter what happens, she puts herself last. When my nan and dad were ill, she didn't hesitate to pause her life to fix mine. And whilst this is one of her many qualities that make her so important to me, I felt a responsibility to make sure that no one took advantage of this trait.

"I think that you have been an amazing friend to Blain and that you deserve to have a few carefree weeks enjoying yourself with your best friend. And I hope he appreciates your patience and love for him," I said.

A smile formed on her pretty face. "He does. I know he does."

Brannon

We waited for Blain and his nan at reception. Any minute now, he would arrive, and I'd be reunited with my best friend.

People started to walk through, carrying their luggage with them and lining up at the reception desk. Asher was welcoming the guests and offering out his help if it was needed. His dad felt it important for him to start doing these things, and when I saw him smartly dressed in his suit and tie, I immediately agreed.

Every face that wasn't Blain's made the wait feel longer. But then, as I saw the ink black hair, styled to perfection, I felt myself running towards him. I threw my arms around his neck as he dropped his bags and did the same back. We embraced the warmth and love of each other in a hug that lasted forever. Emotions erupted within me and I felt my eyes well with tears. A part of me had been missing without Blain, and I was so happy to have that part of me back.

He wiped away the tears that ran down my face.

"Don't cry, Bran!" he said.

"I've missed you so much, Blain."

"I've missed you, too."

After a second long hug, I greeted his nan.

"Hi, Silvia. It's so good to see you!" I said.

"Hello, Brannon. Good to see you, too," she said.

Immediately, I knew that she wasn't overly keen on seeing me. She seemed uneasy and stared at me like I was someone to be wary of. I wasn't used to this. She was normally very welcoming and friendly. I'd known her all my life.

"I've already collected your key from reception, so you don't have to queue up," I said, passing them their key card. "I'll show you where it is and leave you to unpack."

"Thanks, Bran. You're amazing," Blain said.

"It's getting late so how about you come to mine for breakfast? I'll show you where it is on the way."

Blain looked at his nan, and she didn't look pleased with this idea. I felt uncomfortable. Blain's nan wasn't usually like this.

"We'll be there," Blain said.

I walked them to their cabin, helping them with their luggage.

"Where is Mr Curator?" Silvia asked after what felt like a long walk in silence.

"You can call him Asher. He's working tonight. He's seeing the other guests into their cabins," I told her.

She nodded. The silence continued.

I carried their bags into the entrance of the cabin and left them for the night. Blain stepped outside to say goodnight.

"Thank you so much for your help tonight, Bran. I'm excited to have a gossip tomorrow!" he said.

"Me too, I really have missed you so much. But, Blain, is your nan okay? Have I said something wrong?" I asked, worried that she disliked me after this time apart.

It was weird feeling someone else's emotions. But I felt Blain's guilt and I could tell that his answer was likely to be full of dishonesty.

"Don't worry, Bran! She's just tired. We've been travelling all day. She'll be happier tomorrow."

Asher

Blain's nan was not happier tomorrow.

Brannon told me everything that had happened since Blain arrived. The hug they shared after months apart, the fact that they were happy with their luxury cabin that my dad had gifted them for their stay and that Silvia had been incredibly off with Brannon. She also told me about Blain's emotions that she felt last night, which increased my suspicions even more.

They came to Brannon's cabin for breakfast, where she had laid out a spread of fresh pastries, bowls of colourful fruits and countless fillings.

We sat around her breakfast bar, enjoying the food and appreciating the effort she had made.

I think Blain became aware of my concerns almost instantly. I was already at Brannon's cabin when he arrived. I greeted him with a smile and a hug but struggled to reciprocate his enthusiasm over seeing me.

"So, Asher, how has it been, practically living with Brannon?" Blain asked, sharing an excitement between himself and Brannon.

"No complaints from my end. She's incredible. And so is our life together," I said, winking across the table at Brannon.

Silvia coughed and placed her cutlery down.

"Feel free to take some more, Silvia," Brannon politely said.

"I'm fine, thank you," she replied, with the same fake smile that she had worn the entire morning.

Blain didn't comment on his nan's behaviour. He barely mentioned her at all after she had left.

We took Blain on a walk after breakfast to see the newly installed pool and waterfall, and the rest of the changes to the camp.

"I can't believe how different life was when I was last here," Blain said as we strolled past the busy beach.

"I know," Brannon said, "everything has changed."

"You can say that again," Blain spoke under his breath.

"Aside from the obvious, what else has changed in your life Blain?" I asked him.

"Oh, nothing," he replied, bluntly.

I gave him a look of disbelief. I felt like something wasn't right and I still couldn't understand how he could go back to being normal with Brannon after not speaking to her for so long.

"We thought you would've visited sooner. Free holidays all year round, now," I said, trying to make light of this conversation that I desperately wanted to have.

Brannon looked concerned. She could tell I felt uneasy and was digging for an answer.

"Well, things haven't been easy since we lost my grandad," Blain said.

I immediately felt guilty for making him bring it up, and thought to apologise, but he was still speaking.

"My nan has needed company. It's brought us even closer together than we were before his death."

"She's really lucky to have you. How are you feeling about it all now?" Brannon asked, offering some comfort to her best friend.

"Much better. I've accepted it and learnt so much more about my family since he left us. I feel like my nan wouldn't have opened up to me how she has done if he was still alive. I guess he was the one she spoke to about stuff."

"It's good to find the positives in such horrible situations and focus on them," Brannon said.

"What sort of stuff have you found out, then?" I asked.

Blain shot me a look of confusion. Or realisation. Why was I asking? What did I expect to hear? Why won't I be normal with him?

"When my nan tells me that it's okay to share, I will. I don't want to discuss it without her permission. I hope you can understand that," he said.

"Of course we can, Blain. It isn't mine or Asher's business anyway," Brannon said, her eyes telling me to stop whatever it is I'm trying to do.

I stopped after that. I didn't want to upset her; I just couldn't help myself. When I initially met Blain, I had instantly liked him, and I very quickly respected him. The thought of him being deceitful and distant was hard for me to accept. He and Brannon were inseparable. Everything I told her I knew would be relayed to him. They represented everything that best friends should be. I couldn't help but feel like there was more to his disappearance and silence.

Brannon

Asher announced that he had to go meet his dad and work for the rest of the day. He hadn't told me this information, however I could tell through the ability of my powers that he was angry. What he was angry at, I wasn't sure.

Blain and I sat on the edge of the pool, facing the waterfall and admiring its elegance. I felt so lucky to be sitting with my best friend again.

"Are you missing your mum?" Blain asked.

"Of course. I miss her and Marley every day. But, when I went back to Heston for a few weeks, it didn't feel like home anymore," I said.

Blain looked down, trying to hide the guilt in his eyes that I already knew was there. He placed his hand on mine.

"I'm so sorry that I didn't come to your dad's funeral," he said.

I don't know what I expected him to feel guilty about, but it wasn't that.

"Blain, don't be silly. We were both going through so much. I would never have expected you to have come."

"I know, but it must've been so hard. And I wasn't there to support you," he said, continuing to apologise.

"I had my family around me. And anyway, I wasn't good company."

He smiled lovingly and I thought, you're here now. That's all I care about.

"I heard through Heston gossip that you ended up staying with your mum for quite a while. What was that for?" Blain asked.

Something about his question felt strange. It didn't feel like our usual friendly catch-up questions. It felt calculated, in some way. Like Blain expected a certain answer from me.

"No reason, I just wanted to spend some time with mum and Marley before moving to camp permanently," I lied.

He pretended to believe me, which was an even stranger feeling. We'd never pretended anything with each other before.

"Oh, I see. Good idea," he said.

I felt an awkwardness falling over us. I needed to make conversation.

"Asher loved Heston," I said, attempting an enthusiastic tone of voice.

"I knew he would," Blain said. "It's just like a more historic, colder version of here."

I laughed.

"You've never been interested in history, how would you know?" I said, joking back.

"I'm not interested in history."

Blain's sudden transition from joking around to being bluntly defensive welcomed the awkwardness back. This time, I couldn't think of anything to say to break the mood. I didn't think that suggesting someone's interest in history would be taken in such an accusatory way.

"Asher seems different to how he was last summer, when I was here," Blain said.

"In what way?" I asked, glad that the silence was over.

"He doesn't seem as laid back. He seems very tense. He definitely doesn't seem to like me as much."

I paused. Asher had been acting off with Blain. It annoyed me that he had made Blain feel disliked.

"Don't be silly, of course he still likes you. He's doing a lot of work at the moment. I bet it's just stressing him out a bit."

I was glad that Blain didn't have the same powers as me. He couldn't tell the feelings of another. He couldn't feel the guilt oozing out of my every word as I lied to him.

Asher

I visited Brannon's cabin later on in the evening. She had just finished her dinner and was watching TV when I walked in. I kissed her on the head. "Hello, gorgeous. How was your day?" I asked, falling on the couch beside her.

She paused the TV.

"It was good, thank you. How was yours?" she asked, in a standoffish way.

"It was fine, thanks. Did you get up to much with Blain?"

"We went in the new pool. I showed him around a little bit more. Then he went to see his nan," she said.

"Sounds fun. What are we watching?"

She said nothing, but I knew we were about to disagree on something because I purposely saw it in the future. But, unfortunately for me, knowing it was coming didn't mean I could prevent it.

"You didn't go to work today, did you Asher?" she asked.

"Bran, I can explain that."

The purple pools of her eyes were not glistening at me. They were brewing with anger, something that Brannon struggled to control.

"I wish you would," she said.

"Okay, well, to be honest, I don't feel very comfortable about you and Blain's friendship right now," I admitted.

She laughed. I didn't expect that kind of reaction.

"You're joking, right? You can't seriously be jealous over Blain!"

Now I was laughing, too. She can't seriously think I would get jealous over her and her gay best friends' relationship.

"Of course I'm not!" I said. "I'm just concerned about his actions. One minute he didn't want to know you. Now, in a matter of a day, he has travelled to Greece to see you. It's too quick of a change for me, Brannon."

"What are you suggesting, Asher? That he wants something from me?" she asked, her frustration at my accusation displaying itself.

"Maybe. I don't know. I want to protect you and look out for you. And, with that being said, it's going to take a little bit more than breakfast to convince me that he has rekindled your friendship for the right reasons," I said, feeling as though my point was valid.

She looked disbelievingly at me.

"I can't believe your telling me that you think Blain has bad intentions. We have been friends for as long as I can remember. We both went through a bad time and needed our own space. Now, we are both healing, and would like to be in each other's company again. Why is that such a problem for you?" she said, her voice growing louder with every word.

I get why she was angry. I was accusing her best friend, the person she had made the majority of her memories with, of being less than the incredible person that she believed him to be. That I believed him to be. I wished that I could feel as excited to spend time with him. I see him as a good friend, as well. He helped me show Brannon how much I loved her, and we built a brotherly relationship in her absence when her father passed. But it was pointless hiding my suspicion over his actions. If I didn't tell her, she'd venture into my emotions and find out herself. This disagreement was completely unavoidable.

"Brannon, I'm sorry. Look, I don't want to upset you. Maybe I should talk to Blain tomorrow. He might be able to reassure me. How does that sound?" I asked, hoping she would instantly fall back into the old, much calmer, Brannon.

"You can do what you want, but whatever you are trying to accuse Blain of, it won't be true."

"You're probably right," I said, and the thing is, she normally was.

"I'm going to bed," she said.

"Shall I come with you?" I asked.

"No, I'd like to be alone tonight, thanks."

Brannon

Maybe it was harsh, but I didn't want to spend the night with Asher. He had made me so angry that I couldn't bear to fake being okay with him. Blain and I have always been extremely protective of one another, like brother and sister. My love for Asher, and there's a lot of it, doesn't change that.

I struggled to sleep, tossing and turning with thoughts of Asher seeing Blain in a negative light. Confused as to why he seemed to have a lack of trust in him. I have an abundance of trust for Blain. But I also trust Asher, with my life, which made this even more confusing.

I got up early and went for a lengthy walk up the mountain. I sat on a lookout, watching the sunrise.

The sun pushed its way through a cluster of clouds, making them glow as it rose. In no time at all, rays of golden sunlight shot through the sky. The sight of it calmed me. My mind, rather than twisting around bad thoughts, became still as I appreciated the beauty of life.

The water beneath glistened. The sun transformed the colour of the sea from navy blue to turquoise. I was very fond of this colour. I saw it every time I looked into Asher's eyes.

Asher

I woke up from a lonely night's sleep and knew my plan straight away. I messaged Blain, asking him to meet me for breakfast in the canteen.

He was waiting for me when I arrived. His black hair was gelled neatly into place, making me look as if I'd just rolled out of a bush with my nest of chestnut curls.

"Good morning," he said as I sat down opposite him.

"How are you?" I asked him.

"So glad to be waking up here again."

I smiled. Compliments about camp always meant a lot to me. "Is your nan okay? I know I've only met her once, but she seemed a little off," I said.

"Oh, Asher. How I have missed your unfiltered honesty," Blain said, and I wasn't sure if this was a good or bad thing.

"Well, I've got nothing to hide," I joked, analysing his reaction to my words.

"My nan is usually quiet. She doesn't enjoy travelling much. And before you ask why I brought her with me if she doesn't like travelling, I couldn't leave her on her own. She doesn't cope well without my grandad."

A part of me regretted being so weary of Blain. Speaking to him in this way reminded me of our friendship. Sheer honesty and his ability to know what I'm about to say before I say it.

Blain had taken the time to get to know me. He never shrugged me off as his best friend's boyfriend. He included me and made an effort with me. Equally, I did with him too, which is why I know I'm not being paranoid in thinking that something doesn't feel right.

"I'm sorry to hear about the loss of your grandad. I wish me and Brannon could've been there for you more," I said.

He took a sip of his water before replying.

"That's fine. I wanted to be alone," he said.

During summer camp, Blain had never been this blunt. In fact, I've never known someone with the ability to talk as much as he can. His quietness since being here didn't reassure me in the slightest.

"Brannon isn't too pleased with me right now," I told him.

"Why? What have you done?"

I sensed anger in his voice. Brannon and he were as equally protective of one another.

"I suggested that your actions seem a little bit suspicious."

From the shocked look on his face I could tell that had taken him aback. He hadn't expected me to say that and he stayed quiet for a long moment. Minutes passed. I waited.

"What...I mean why...what would...why do you think that?" he asked, struggling to form a sentence, like someone would if they were under pressure.

"I just find it all a bit sudden," I said. "You hadn't spoken to Brannon properly for months. You didn't see her before she moved here. You didn't answer her phone calls. She's been really sad without you." His eyes became teary. "And then, suddenly, you are up for visiting camp and travelling across Europe with your nan to see her. It doesn't make sense."

Blain let out a deep sigh. I wish Brannon was here to tell me how he felt, but if I had to guess I would say he felt disappointed. In himself. He had let down someone who wouldn't dream of treating him how he had treated her.

"I get it. I haven't been a good friend to Brannon recently. And you have every right to feel how you do. My actions don't look sincere, and I wish I could explain why. It's hard to find the words." He paused for a moment, looking into my eyes. He continued again. "Asher, I need you to believe that I would never intentionally hurt Brannon. She's like my sister. Literally the most amazing person to bless my life. Things have been, well, different lately. But I'm back now and I won't let her down again."

For some reason beyond my knowledge, I believed him. Words can be planned but emotions are harder to fake, and I could hear the regret in his voice. He really did feel bad for disappearing on her. He really did feel guilty for not talking to her. And, most importantly, he really did still love her.

Although my suspicions were still there, I didn't feel the need to question him anymore. The reasoning behind his behaviour seemed private and I would never force him to tell me his business. I only cared about his intentions with Brannon, and if they were to disappear again after this holiday, then I wouldn't forgive him.

"What about when you're in Heston and she's here with me? Are you going to still be her friend?" I asked.

"Of course. I've missed her as well, Asher. My life has been empty without her," he said, and I could imagine that life would indeed feel extremely empty without her.

"I'll assume that you've also missed me and that you can't imagine a life without me, too," I said, lifting the very heavy atmosphere from around us.

Blain laughed.

"Yes, Asher, if you like."

"Good. Well, I think it's best you come with me to find Brannon. She'll forgive me if she sees you there, too."

He laughed again before standing up and joining me.

"We aren't going to her cabin, by the way. I've already checked, and she isn't there," I said.

"Where is she then?" he asked.

"My guess is as good as yours, but let's start with the mountain walk."

Brannon

I noticed their smiling faces walking towards me and instantly felt a burst of happiness.

Asher's chat with Blain appeared to have cleared things up. I heard them joking together in the distance before they saw me. I had felt annoyed at Asher all morning but seeing my two favourite people together melted my frustration away.

Blain ran up to me, opening his arms wide for a hug.

"Good morning my beautiful best friend," he said.

I looked to Asher who wasn't being as confident as Blain. He felt worried. Worried that I hadn't forgiven him yet.

"Good morning, Bran," he said in a timid tone.

"Good morning," I replied.

"Look, you two, I haven't travelled this many miles and climbed a whole mountain to not witness the extraordinary love story of Mr Curator and Miss Amory. Sort it out, guys," Blain said, sounding much more like himself and word vomiting his thoughts.

A smile broke across my face. Of course I forgave him. Asher threw himself at me, squeezing me into his chest. I giggled. This was my favourite type of hug, and he knew it.

"I love you, Bran," Asher said.

"I love you," I said back.

"And suddenly normality resumes. You two go back to being your loved-up selves and I go back to my pit of jealousy," Blain said.

We all laughed and began to plan the rest of our day.

Asher

It was lovely to see Brannon and Blain back together in full force. But, although Blain and I had smoothed things over, he didn't seem as himself with me just yet.

Brannon wanted to go for a picnic on the pier for lunch. She prepared chicken sandwiches and chocolate dipped strawberries for us to eat. She invited Silvia, Blain's nan, but she didn't want to come.

The sun was scorching. The aquamarine surface of the ocean was hard to see with all the surfers, swimmers and inflatable unicorn dinghies.

Brannon was glowing. Her tanned skin looked golden in the sunlight, and her hair fell down her back in velvety purple waves. It was like a reward, seeing her beautiful smile and hearing her laugh. Not a day goes by without me thanking the universe for gifting me with a real-life angel.

I left around 3pm to help the kitchen staff with the dinner buffet. Brannon said they were going to get a double seat inflatable from her cabin and relax in the sea.

Brannon

Feeling the soft waves lift the inflatable was a motion I had missed. Blain and I had always talked about the day when we would have total freedom, exploring the world on brightly coloured inflatables and sipping cocktails as we talked about anything best friends would talk about. It felt like, after everything we had been through, that day had finally come.

"I think I could stay here forever," Blain said, splashing his feet around in the clear water.

"I am going to stay here forever. And can you blame me?" I said, before taking another sip of my pineapple and mango drink.

"Certainly not. If I could live in a place like this with a boyfriend like yours, I don't think I'd ever complain again," he said, which made me chuckle.

He was right. I was more than lucky to live here. I was equally, if not more, lucky to have Asher here too.

"What were you and Asher doing together this morning?" I asked.

I noticed Blain tense up slightly at this question.

"He wanted to talk to me," he said.

His honey-soaked eyes, lit up by the sun, stared into the sea.

"About?" I asked, mistaken in thinking he would explain without the extra nudge.

"He felt like I disappeared and reappeared too quickly," he said.

"Oh, right. He's just looking out for me, I think. I told him he was being stupid, though. You wouldn't be here for the wrong reasons."

Blain didn't respond as quickly as I expected. He smiled, but it wasn't a confident or reassuring smile. I felt the atmosphere cloud with guilt again.

"He was looking out for you, yes. I'd never seen him like that before, other than the time that Dylan boy was trying to force you to drink alcohol. He was very stern, very straight to the point," Blain said.

"Asher does have that side to him. You're probably used to his soft side when he's around me. But he doesn't mess about," I said. "When I first met him, I remember feeling intimidated by his presence. Obviously, it was because I fancied him, but I can imagine he comes across quite upfront."

"Yeah, that's one word for it."

The conversation fell dead after that. It was as if bringing up Asher was the same as pressing a pause button on our friendship. It had been the opposite at summer camp, when Blain was helping Asher set a picnic up for me, or when he was doing my hair for the summer ball.

I couldn't think of anything to say. We were bobbing up and down on a giant inflatable float, in silence, listening to the chatter and laughter of everyone around us. A bigger wave rocked us and Blain tipped sideways a little. A glint of metal shone at his neck.

"What's that?" I asked, pointing to the necklace that was reflecting the sunlight.

Without a second thought, Blain covered the necklace with his hand.

"Oh, nothing. Just something my nan gave me."

I wouldn't have thought anything of it if his reaction hadn't been so quick to conceal whatever his nan's gift had been. My effort levels were running low. It was impossible to talk to him, my best friend of eighteen years. And it was really starting to hurt.

"I should get back to my nan. She'll be wondering when dinner is," Blain said.

I nodded in agreement, feeling defeated. After Asher had cleared the air with him, I assumed things would go back to normal. And they had, for a short while. But Blain wasn't being himself with me. I kept hitting a nerve with him that meant he became distant and closed off from me. In this moment, I didn't know what to do, and I struggled to recognise the boy sitting beside me.

Asher

I managed to escape from the evening shift on camp. As soon as Brannon told me that she was upset about Blain, I knew where I needed to be. She's my priority. Now. Tomorrow. Forever.

I walked in to find her bundled up on the sofa, with dull eyes and red cheeks.

"Hey, gorgeous," I said.

"Hey," she replied, sounding flat.

"What happened?" I asked.

"The same as yesterday. Blain wasn't himself with me again. I don't know what else to say or do to fix it because I don't know what there is to fix. I assumed we would be fine. We don't seem fine," she explained, and I could hear the ball in her throat tightening as she struggled to get the words out.

"It's a difficult one, isn't it? I'm not too sure what to suggest, to be honest. If you'd done something wrong, I would tell you so you can make it better again. But you've done nothing wrong to Blain. You've given him time to grieve, you've been patient with him, you've waited for months to get your best friend back. I'm just so sorry that it isn't going how we'd have hoped," I said, attempting to comfort her.

Since I met her, Brannon has always been a very emotional person. She doesn't hide how she feels or try to stop herself from feeling things and she feels everything, in detail.

"I feel bad. He's flown out here to see me and I don't even know what to do with him tomorrow because it will just end in an awkward silence," she said.

"It's not your fault, Brannon. Please don't blame yourself."

She didn't respond.

"Maybe let him and his nan make their own plans tomorrow. I'll keep you busy," I told her.

She nodded and tried to smile, but I didn't need her emotionally invasive powers to know that her smile was insincere.

I squeezed next to her on the couch and hugged her until her eyes began to flicker shut. Then I suggested we head to bed.

We lay in her bed, which smelt as it always did of floral, fresh linen.

"Things will get better. They always do," I said, kissing her head.

"I know," she said.

I held her gently until her breathing stilled and she drifted off to sleep. My heart was breaking for her and I had no idea how I could get Blain to be more honest with us.

Brannon

I woke at 4am needing to use the bathroom. I gently lifted Asher's arms off me, desperately trying not to wake him up.

Tip-toeing to the door and pulling my dressing gown from the hook, I closed the door after me, gently releasing the handle back into place before glancing down the corridor to the kitchen and living room. A light was on. I never leave the lights on after going to bed, but I had been tired when Asher had guided me into the bedroom.

I walked down the corridor. The sofa looked the same, just as we had left it. The pots and pans were drying on the draining board, just how I'd left them. The TV was turned off, but the lamp on the sideboard was turned on. I didn't think we'd even had that lamp on last night.

I wandered over, thinking that the electricity might have tripped and turned it on. Or maybe Asher had come back to this room for something and forgot to turn it off after him. It wasn't a big deal. Until I saw what the lamp was spotlighting.

Panic raced through my bones. Right in front of me, the words.

They'd been strategically placed. Not by me or Asher. Someone else had been in here.

They had caused me stress for weeks and as anxiety pumped through my bloodstream, I remembered that feeling very well.

They ran through my head every day. They left me with questions that I had no idea how to answer. Every morning I concluded that, if anything, they owed me so much sleep.

My chest was tight. My breathing felt restricted. I couldn't peel my eyes away from the sight of them. I tried to form a word but it wouldn't come. I forced myself to draw a breath and shouted, as loud as I ever had, "Asher!"

We looked everywhere for answers. What did the words mean? Why were they left for me? What did the stranger want me to know?

I knew none of the answers. But I no longer had to worry about the stranger. They weren't a stranger anymore.

The words, the ones that came with every object that Juno had me find, were laid out under the glow of the lamp, the upturned corners of the scraps of paper casting shadows underneath.

If only you knew ... it started with me.

And the necklace that I spotted around Blain's neck, lying next to them.

Asher

I woke up instantly when Brannon shouted my name. The thought of her being in danger forced me out of bed quicker than my mind could register what was happening.

I raced down the corridor to find her, but she didn't look like she was in danger. She wasn't crying. There was no sign of injury. She was simply standing there. Looking at the surface of her sideboard, where the lamp was turned on.

"What's up, Bran? The way you shouted, I'd have thought there was someone else in here," I said.

Her gaze shot towards me. Her eyes were frozen in shock.

"There was."

"What do you mean?"

"Come and look for yourself."

I couldn't imagine what had caused her to act like this. I couldn't think of anything that would be on her sideboard to scare her this much. But I understood as soon as I saw them.

The words that had been haunting her. The scraps of paper that had reassured her that the objects she found were the correct ones. She hadn't got them out for weeks. She could no longer bare the sight of them. Someone else had put them there, in the correct order, forming the sentence that we had been wondering about for ages.

"What's this?" I said, picking up the necklace that was left beside the words.

"I noticed it today," she said. "Blain was wearing it."

Every possible thought of why these words were here disappeared from my head instantly, as if Brannon's words had pushed them off a towering cliff to their death. Blain's necklace? With the words? Nothing made sense.

I had no reassuring words of comfort for Brannon, or for myself. In fact, no words came out of my mouth at all. For the following few minutes, I mirrored Brannon, and stared at the display in front of us. This game of words just got messier. And there was no way that we could ignore this.

Brannon

"I don't know what to say," Asher eventually managed.

In a situation where my mind should be spiralling with uncontrollable thoughts, it was quiet. I didn't know what to think. There weren't words adequate for my thoughts to form in a way they could describe how I felt.

"So it was Blain?" I finally said, trying to process the situation out loud.

"Can we make assumptions like that?" Asher asked.

"Well, it's his necklace. I saw him wearing it today. His nan gave it to him."

"His nan who has been incredibly off with us and locked herself away in her cabin for the past two days?" Asher asked, sarcastically.

"Yes, that one."

I looked at the scraps of paper with the words scrawled on them, reading them over and over again in their intended order.

"If only you knew...it started with me." I kept repeating the words to Asher.

"What does that even mean? What started?" Asher questioned.

"I don't know," I answered, my mind still fighting to make sense of any of it.

I picked up the necklace. Its silver coating looked rusted. Then it hit me.

"Asher," I said. "Look at it. What does the symbol look like to you?"

"I'm not sure. I mean, it looks a little bit like our pendants. Just less circular, I guess," he said, not catching on.

"Asher, it's a crescent."

"Like a moon?" he asked.

"Like a moon," I repeated.

I untucked my pendant and Asher copied. I held them together, creating a full circle, like the symbol on the bracelet that Asher gifted me.

"I recognise these symbols," Asher said.

"Me too. They were imprinted on some of the objects. The rings. The candle."

"A sun and a moon," Asher said, analysing our pendants and Blain's necklace.

"The Sol and Lunar witches," I said. "The ones Juno didn't want to tell us about."

We looked at each other in disbelief. The dots were connecting. Yet still we had no answers.

Asher

The sky was getting lighter, and the sun was beginning to dapple through Brannon's curtains. It surprised me when I saw the time and realised we'd been standing in shock and confusion for nearly an hour already.

The adrenaline that pulsed through my body meant that I felt no trace of the shock and fear I'd initially felt when Brannon shouted my name at 4am. I felt wide awake, full of energy and desperate to see Blain. To know if it was him all along.

"I'm going to take a shower," Brannon said, and walked out of the room.

I decided to distract myself and started to tidy up the room. Fluffing the pillows on the sofa, I put them in their place. I put away the washing from last night. Then I saw, on the island in the middle of the kitchen, Brannon's handbag.

Everything that had been in it was now placed around it. Her receipts were spread across the surface, her lip gloss thrown to the side and her purse, that had clearly been searched through, left unzipped beside it. Of course. She kept the words in her purse. Whoever it was, likely to be Blain, was desperate to find these words. So desperate that they had searched through Brannon's things.

Another question came to my mind. How did they get in?

I made my way around the house, checking the windows and doors. The front door was locked, I remembered doing it the night before. The windows were all locked, too. But the back door to the garden was open.

Brannon returned from her shower as I was shutting the back door, locking it this time. She'd thrown on the first vest top and shorts she could find, but she still looked perfect. Her hair was dripping onto her bronze skin.

"Did I leave the back door open?" she asked, placing a hand over her mouth.

"Yes, I think so," I said, trying not to make her feel guilty.

"Damn it! I always forget to lock the back door." She paused. "Blain would know that."

"I should have checked too," I offered. "Why don't you go dry your hair? You'll get a cold if you leave it wet," I said, trying to shield her from her empty handbag and the belongings scattered over the surface.

But it was too late. She saw it.

"What's this?" she asked, picking up her stuff and looking through it all as if it didn't belong to her.

"Well, you leave the words in your purse, don't you?"

"He looked through my stuff!" she exclaimed, instantly angry and clearly confident that this was Blain's doing.

"Don't worry, I'll sort this out. You get yourself sorted. Then we'll go to his cabin," I said.

"Yes, we will be going to his cabin. I'll give him his necklace back," she said before storming out.

It was obvious that she didn't feel anything but rage right now. She wanted to find Blain and question him. She wanted answers.

Brannon

Asher took a shower and got dressed after me. He had sorted my entire cabin as well as himself whilst I tried to find the patience to wait and not make my own way to Blain's.

As soon as he was ready, we left, anger motivating my every step.

We got to the door of the cabin quickly. I knocked. His nan answered the door.

"Oh, good. We've been waiting for you," she said, moving out of the way so that we could come in.

Silvia threw me off slightly. I didn't know whether to be angry or confused. But one question was immediately answered; this was definitely to do with Blain.

Blain was sitting on a chair at the kitchen table, unable to look up from his hands. Asher and I sat opposite while Silvia took the seat next to him. Suddenly, my anger wasn't enough. I didn't know what to say.

Luckily, Silvia had found her voice.

"I've made a pot of tea," she said, like it would help to calm the rising tension around the table. "I understand that you probably both have questions for Blain. You might be feeling angry at him. But I want you to know that I have asked him to do everything that he has done. Please, blame me," she said.

Her black hair, threaded with several strands of grey streaks, rested perfectly behind her ears. It was short and curly, offering some youth to her wrinkled face. Her eyes were a dark hazel, like Blain's, and she had thin, pale lips. I'd been to her house many times and she'd seen me grow from a toddler to an adult. But, sitting in front of her right now, I felt like we barely knew each other at all.

The thought of her and Blain knowing about my episodes and the Myst was unbelievable, but it seemed they must. Somehow, she knew I had been on a supernatural treasure hunt, because the words were left by her.

"It's hard to know where to start," Asher said.

Silvia placed her hand on his, the first act of kindness she'd performed since being here. Asher looked surprised.

"Was it you?" I asked, looking directly at Blain.

It didn't feel like I was looking at my best friend. The loud, bubbly, honest friend who I trusted with every ounce of my being. Asher's suspicions were right. Now the person sitting in front of me was a liar.

"Yes," Blain said. "I made sure that you found every object. And I left the words with them."

Silence. I didn't believe him. I couldn't.

"Let me explain," Silvia said. "Now, where do I begin?"

Me and Asher shared a look of concern. How could she possibly explain this?

Asher

Silvia began to explain in her raspy, deep voice. No one would have needed to see the pack of cigarettes on the kitchen counter to tell that she was a smoker.

"When my husband died, I had no one to discuss the supernatural world with. I'd always believed that Blain should be told about the family's history, but his grandad, understandably, didn't think he'd take it seriously enough. So, we never told him." She took a sip of her tea. "Brannon, I've known your family since long before your parents were even born. We are very few of the witching families that remained in Heston. It was only by luck that you and Blain became best friends, and I can assure you that a friendship like yours cannot be faked."

Brannon looked at Blain, rage still burning in her eyes. Blain looked at Brannon, guilt and sorrow seeping over the edges.

"It was only after I read Blain's letter that I understood the summer camp that the school was sending you to was owned by a family with the surname Curator. I knew then that I would have to intervene. Blain told me that you weren't keen on the idea of camp. It didn't look like you were going to go, so I made sure that he encouraged you. Pressured you, even. I told him that you'd never get another chance to make memories like this together, and that was enough for him to nag you into agreeing.

"It was essential that you met Asher, Brannon. Even if you didn't fall deeply in love, I wanted you to have the chance to see for yourself. The pendant owners before you didn't meet, so had no choice but to throw it away on their eighteenth birthday. With your school offering to take you to this summer camp, it was too much of a coincidence. You two were meant to meet. Fate deemed it right."

I smiled at Brannon. It was true. We were meant to meet, meant to be, meant to love each other. Whether it was planned or natural, I'd never regret meeting her.

Silvia continued.

"I was overjoyed when Blain told me that you and Asher were in love. I knew that you had kept the pendants as soon as Blain told me that Asher was coming to Heston once camp finished. I figured that this was because you could no longer be apart. Every family with a history of witches, vampires and wolves felt a change in the wind. And it was a truly wonderful thing to know that any passing of a supernatural bloodline would end up in the magical afterlife of the Myst."

"So, all this time, you knew why I fainted randomly?" Brannon asked.

"Yes, and I was the one who made sure that Blain never worried or asked questions," Silvia said.

Brannon nodded but didn't reply.

"You must remember this, Brannon. I've only ever wanted the best for you. I still do. I just didn't know how else to handle this," Silvia explained. "Anyway, it was when Blain told me that Asher's family were becoming severely ill that I linked their suffering to your father's death. I've studied witchcraft since I was a child, I recognised that the power wasn't settling properly, so it was looking for a home in an incapable body. Quickly, I figured that only one person could fix this. Juno."

"How did you know about the objects and where I'd be sent to find them?" Brannon asked.

"My family have been collecting magical objects for centuries. We knew that one day we would need them if we wanted Juno's full power to return. It's also, obviously, a big interest of mine. As for knowing where to place them, the witching community often failed to display the quality of being trustworthy. Juno had told Ancestors who she believed to be close to her about the things in her notepad. The objects that would one day be required to manipulate the spell of the Myst. The places where they were hidden. The people she trusted to deliver them if they were ever needed. And the great thing about these witching families is that they couldn't move location. Juno would be dead and unable to communicate with them. She needed to know that they would be in the same place as she'd written in that notepad. In fact, they swore an oath for it."

"So you knew that Mrs Westman had that necklace and that she lived in Heston still?" Brannon asked.

"Yes. I made a conscious effort to continue my families doings and keep in contact with the nearby witching families," Silvia said.

Brannon

Silvia's explanation, so far, made sense. But it was a lot to take in. And I didn't know how to feel about it.

"I managed to arrange all of the objects and the words, with Blain helping to deliver the physical demands of the challenge. Soon enough, you had the objects and returned to Greece. You'd let Blain know, despite his silence, that Asher's family were better, and I knew that my job was done. I had left my imprint on you by leaving the words," Silvia finished.

"Why didn't you tell me any of this?" I asked Blain, feeling a sense of betrayal from my best friend.

"I made him promise not to tell you anything," Silvia said.

Apparently, Blain had lost the ability to talk.

"Why?" I asked, directing my question to Blain again.

"I didn't know my next steps, and you knowing what I was up to may have meant that you stopped doing it. There were too many risks involved with you knowing and it was easier if you didn't," Silvia said.

"Easier for you, yes," I said. "Not easier for anyone else."

"Actually, I think this made it easier for Blain, too. He barely understood himself, he wouldn't have been able to relay all of this information to you, as well," Silvia said.

"Fine. What is it that you're up to then? Why did I need to see those words? What's the point in all of this?" I asked, my anger simmering at the deception.

"My name is Silvia Crescent, descendant of Ancestor Selene Crescent herself. My family are Lunar witches. I needed to get in your head and plant a seed of interest about us. I'm getting old now, as you can see. It's my last chance to change the future of my witching kind."

I stood up and walked out.

Asher

I used my powers to look ahead and see Brannon's next move. She was going to the pier. I guessed that, quite rightly, she felt overwhelmed and needed space to process everything.

"Did I say something wrong?" Silvia asked.

"It's a lot to take in," I said.

"Asher, she needs to believe that I didn't have a choice. She's the first person I wanted to talk to about this," Blain said.

"To be honest, Blain, I don't think she'll care right now. She has just been told that the stranger who left her mysterious words and caused her so much confusion was her best friend, and that his nan is from a Lunar witch family. I mean, we didn't even know about Lunar witches until Brannon had to find the objects. We may be the pendant holders, but your nan probably knows much more about us than we do," I said, being honest with both of them.

"You should probably know that I'm in the same bloodline as my nan," Blain said.

"So, technically, you're a Lunar witch too?" I asked.

"I will be when I die," Blain said, bluntly.

"Listen, I'm going to go see Brannon. I can imagine she needs me. Thanks for the explanation, Silvia, I just wish your plan didn't have to interfere with their friendship," I said.

Neither of them had anything to say in response. I stood up and walked out, knowing where my priorities lay, and that was being with Brannon.

Brannon

The sea was a still blanket of cyan blue. Rays of sunlight attached themselves to the rocky cliffs surrounding the beach. The stretching shore seemed like resin covering the soft, yellow ground. As I sat on the hot wood of the pier, I wondered how anything could be wrong.

"You need to find a new hiding place." My favourite voice. "It's getting too easy to find you."

I didn't turn around, but a smile had crept upon my face. He sat beside me, looking around at the view. I sat looking at him, now wondering whether this view was better. His eyes were the ocean. His skin was the golden sand. His smile was the happiness that anyone would feel here.

"What are you thinking about?" Asher asked.

Him. That's all I was thinking about now.

He approached me with a calm confidence. He knew, whatever the problem was, he'd be able to cheer me up. I think we both found comfort in knowing that even if we couldn't fix each other's problems, we could always make it feel a little easier. He'd hold my hand through it all, and I'd hold his back.

"That's the thing, Asher. There's too much to think about," I said, letting my head fall on his shoulder.

I felt his arm move around my waist and pull me closer to him.

"Let's not think then," he said, as always, suggesting what I needed.

He stood up, held his hand out for me to take, and stood me up with him. We started walking. I didn't know where we were going, but I didn't care. Anywhere with him, I'd go.

Asher

There was no point trying to force her to tell me how she was feeling when she didn't even know herself. The best thing to do, right now, was to distract her. Give her time to process the amount of information we had just been told.

We walked, hands intertwined, down the beach in silence. I wanted to give her mind space, but her heart company.

I directed us to the ice cream parlour and ordered a strawberry and mango scoop. These are her favourite flavours, so she could choose which one she wanted. She chose strawberry, then we set off back to the pier.

After an hour or so of walking, I decided it would be an appropriate time to talk.

We sat back down, her cheek bones glittering in the hot light.

"How was the ice cream?" I asked

"Really good, thank you."

"And how are you feeling?"

"Better."

When she stormed out of Blain's cabin, she was angry. It was clear to me now that she was sad. Overwhelmed with a disappointment that only a best friend can cause.

"Do you want to talk to Blain?" I asked.

"No. Not yet, anyway," she said.

"Why not?"

"I don't know what I would say." She paused. "Is it selfish of me to feel betrayed?"

Typical Brannon. Already trying to blame herself.

"Definitely not," I said.

"I keep thinking that I would never be able to keep a secret from Blain. He's my best friend. I wouldn't want to hide a big thing like that from him." She sighed and looked to the sky, stopping tears from spilling out. "And then I remember that, actually, I have done that. My whole life. Kept a secret from Blain, the biggest part of myself. Not because I didn't want him to know. Of course I did. But besides not being allowed, I was embarrassed. I always saw the supernatural part of me as weird. It's only since I met you that my opinion changed. Now I think that it's the best part of me. Something that makes me interesting. And different."

"Extraordinary. It makes you extraordinary," I told her.

She smiled as a drop of sadness fell from her lilac eyes.

"I'm confused, more than anything. How Silvia and Blain share a bloodline with Lunar witches. That after everything I've done to keep Blain from knowing, he's now in the centre of it. And we could have gone through it together, but instead we kept secrets," she said.

"But Brannon, it's not a bit of gossip that you've purposely hidden from him. Blood runs thicker than water. This was deeper than friendship. It's family," I said.

"I don't think I believe in that. And Blain is family," she said.

"What upset you the most about it?" I asked.

"How it was dealt with. Secrecy is one thing, but to be sly about it is another. The words that Silvia left with the objects have irritated me for so long. I can't even count the hours that

I've thought about who left them and what they meant. It's hard to accept that it was my best friend and his nan that caused me this much unrest," she explained.

It made perfect sense. She didn't feel as though she had the right to be angry at him for keeping a secret from her. Even though keeping secrets isn't their thing, they both have. They kept secrets, for their family's sake. It's the fact that her life has been so unsettled from her time in Heston and to find out that this was caused by one of the only people that she has ever fully trusted is frustrating and hurtful.

Brannon

I can accept that a secret surrounding supernatural happenings has been kept from me. But the answers to all my questions, the information I've spent months looking for and the witching bloodline that I've wanted so desperately to know about have been right in front of me. Avoiding me, sure. But right there.

"What do you want to do about it?" Asher asked.

"I'll talk to Blain tomorrow. I don't feel as though I'm in a good head space to deal with this situation today," I said.

"I think that's a good idea," he said. "Let's get something to eat and then a good night's sleep. I have something planned for tomorrow."

The heat from the sun soaked into my skin and bones and filled my heart with warmth. To describe Asher in one word, he's irresistible. His hair, his eyes, his smile. He's gorgeous. But underneath his appearance is someone who cares so hard for me. Who will do whatever it takes to make me happy. He makes everything feel better. And lighter. He's thoughtful and funny and confident in his ability to show me love.

On our birthdays, when I kept the pendant. When I packed up my life and moved to Greece. On a supernatural treasure hunt to help him and his family. Choosing Asher doesn't come with regrets. And for him, choosing me never comes with hesitation.

He would fly a rocket up to space and steal a piece of the moon. I know he would. Just to see me smile.

Asher

I had to work the night shift with dad, so Brannon spent the night alone. I messaged her to check in, but she went to sleep earlier than normal. After a very early morning, she must have needed the rest. I definitely felt the same.

I knocked on her door late morning, hoping to be greeted with a happier Brannon than yesterday.

"Good morning," happier Brannon said. Her hair was thrown into a messy bun and she was still in her pyjamas.

"Good morning, pretty." I smiled at her. She moved aside to let me in.

"What's the plan for today?" she asked.

"Waiting outside your door," I teased, not wanting to give her an easy answer. "You'll need to wear a swimming costume underneath your clothes. And pass me one of your beach towels."

She walked to her room to get ready. I noticed the shining surfaces of the kitchen and the perfectly positioned pillows and throws over the sofa. I instantly thought back to her house in Heston, and the overwhelming smell of polish when walking in the front door. She got this from her mum. Stress cleaning. Cleaning everything around her as a distraction from the mess in her mind.

"Shall I bring a bag?" she asked, calling out from the bathroom, where she had moved to clean her face.

"No. I'll carry whatever you need to bring," I said, calling back.

It didn't take her long to get ready. Soon enough, she had walked back down the corridor and was asking me more questions, like what food should she bring and how much water should she take. I told her I had sorted it all.

She was wearing a fuchsia pink swimming costume underneath a white vest top and black shorts. She smelt of fruity, floral perfume and the coconut scented sun cream oil that she wore on hot days like this.

"Okay, I'm ready."

Brannon

I couldn't quite believe what I saw when I walked outside. Electric scooters. And Asher smiling, very proudly.

"So," he said, "What do you think?"

I hesitated. "I've never been on one of these before," I said, very unsure about this plan.

"They're easy. Come on, it will be so fun. We can follow the path in the opposite direction to the mountains, go to the rocky bays and see the souvenir shops."

"I haven't explored up there very much," I said.

"It only gets busy at this time of year, for the summer," Asher explained.

I thought about it, still reluctant and with reservations. But he was right, it would be so much fun. "Okay, let's do it."

It took me a while to get used to it. The scooters went faster than I expected. I felt unstable and wobbly for some time before gaining my balance and growing confident with the accelerating handle.

I could tell that Asher wanted to race off, to test how fast these things would go. But he cruised beside me, letting me get used to it.

"Where did you even get these from?" I said, having to raise my voice above the wind that grew stronger as we neared the ocean.

"My dad had the idea to hire them out. He wanted me to trial them, see if they'd be any good," Asher replied.

"I think they'd be popular," I said.

"I think we need to find out how fast they can go," Asher said.

I didn't feel completely confident in my ability to not embarrass myself and tumble off the scooter onto the path, but I knew that Asher wouldn't be able to enjoy himself if I didn't grow the courage to keep up with him. I don't often choose to reminisce on things my dad used to say, simply to avoid upsetting myself. But one of his sayings was repeating in my head. *You can be brave, or you can be comfortable. You can't be both.*

I turned the handle and felt myself jolt forwards. It took me by surprise, but now I was determined to experience this. I pushed the handle even more. I could feel the wind as it whipped my hair. It was more than welcomed, to cool me down in the blazing heat of today.

We followed the brick path, round corners, up and down small hills, and larger ones. To the left of me was the navy ocean, patched with clear turquoise water in places. Large rocks were lined up from the shore to the depths of the sea, only to be seen when the tide was out. They created beautiful bays, where there was less sand than on the main beach. The wind was stronger as we journeyed along the path. The waves round here were much bigger than at the beach we usually went to. The water crashed against the rocks, splashing white froth into the sky. It was a violent act, as the rocks broke the ocean. But there was something so elegant about it. So freeing.

To the right of us, there were fields of vibrantly coloured flowers. Buffaloberry, echinacea purpurea and so many pink flowers that I couldn't tell what they were. Asher's mum, Tammy, once told me about the flowers she enjoyed growing.

The pink flowers always represented Greece to me. The flamingo pink and the azure sea and the white buildings and the baby blue sky. A perfect palette for a perfect painting.

The further along we went, the more buildings came into view. Not the grand, industrial buildings that crowded the sky in cities, but small cocktail huts, and white cobbled shops and bars with spiralling staircases leading to tables on rooftops.

"We aren't in camp anymore," Asher announced.

Camp was a concoction of adventure, serenity and the beauty of nature. This little town had a different feel. A buzz, almost. A radiating happiness to live in such a wonderful place.

There were local people, choosing juicy apricots and the biggest watermelons I'd ever seen from a fruit stall. Their smiles were timeless and youthful. A familiar sight that I often saw on the faces of Heston's locals in summer. It was a feeling that I had carried from there to here. The feeling of never getting fed up with where you live.

There were families on holiday, exploring the many souvenir shops that sold the same thing in every one but were all as equally exciting as the others. There were boards outside the shops, covered in magnets. I guessed that if we had travelled down here on the scooters in the evening, those boards would be less than half full.

"Do you like it?" Asher asked, noticing that I had slowed down to take in my surroundings.

I smiled at him, contently.

"I love it."

Asher

The look on Brannon's face made me question why I never brought her here before. It was as if she was full of life and absorbed by the atmosphere of this little Greek town.

When schools come to camp for the summer, they are restricted to camp premises. We don't arrange trips into town. It's up to the school's staff to do that, and Brannon's school never did.

We'd been swept into supernatural problems since we met. And, unfortunately, it never occurred to me to give Brannon a cultural tour of her new home.

"Are you hungry?" I asked her.

She nodded, refusing to peel her eyes away from the shops.

"Let's park these up and go for a walk," I said.

She followed me to a bit of the path that overlooked the sea. We put the stands on the scooters down and removed the keys. This way, they couldn't be used. Not that I thought anyone would try to steal them anyway.

I took her hand in mine, her skin as soft as a rose petal and her grip gentle.

"This is *i parathalassia poli,*" I told her.

"What does that mean?" she asked.

"The waterfront town."

"It's lovely," she said.

We walked, passing restaurants and bars. The Dolphin Tavern, a cobblestone pub with its sign in a cobalt blue shade. Turtle Shell Cocktail Bar, one of my mum's favourite places to go. Sunset Sky Bar, a rooftop bar, perfect for watching the sun go down. *Troo,* translating to 'eat' in English, one of the best Greek cuisine restaurants. Many of the other restaurants sold mainly English or American inspired dishes. I wanted Brannon to experience Greek food for a change.

"Let's eat in here," I said, directing her in.

I spoke to the waiter, a good friend of my dad's, and he sat us in the window seats with menus.

"Asher," she said, "I don't know what any of this says," Brannon said, closely examining the choice of food.

"Would you trust me to order for you?" I asked.

"Yes, just no fish for me please."

"As if, by now, I wasn't aware that you didn't eat fish," I said.

She laughed before returning her gaze to the happy shoppers strolling past the window.

Food and drink, for us in Greece, is just as important as the stories of Gods. Our culture is what makes us so memorable. Living at camp sometimes keeps me from it, because not everyone wants to experience the country, they just want a relaxing holiday. We have to provide food that the majority of people will eat, and drinks that are recognised by everyone. Whilst Zeus and Apollo, Athena and Hades are hung on the walls in tapestries or their faces are decorating the walls in tiles, it is not in everyone's interest to learn about them. It's always been important for camp to provide a holiday, not a lifestyle.

That aside, this was Brannon's home now. And, by the looks of things, she was desperate to embrace Greek culture.

I ordered two Retsina wines, two shots of Metaxa Brandy, a Pastitsio, a Greek lasagne, Souvlaki, otherwise known as Gyros, a couple of Tomato keftedes, tomato fritters, and Tzatziki, a Greek dip made of yoghurt, garlic, olive oil and cucumber. This was a lot of food for two people, but I decided that Brannon should try multiple dishes. This and the fact that I got over excited about showing Brannon the food I'd grown up eating.

When it arrived, Brannon looked amazed.

"Wow," she said, "it smells incredible."

I handed her some cutlery and we dug in, eating a bit of everything. She loved it all, especially the Gyros.

"I've never had such tasty food. The flavours are just...wow," she said.

"I know right. I'm just sorry I never showed it to you before," I said.

She smiled.

"I think it's fair to say we've been occupied. With another life. Where there's witches and vampires and Juno," she said, laughing gently.

I smiled back, before passing her one of the shots.

"Okay, time for a Metaxa," I said.

We hit the glasses together before pouring the liquid into our mouths. She screwed up her face with the intensity of the drink whilst I attempted to take it like a pro.

"I prefer the Retsina," she said, and I was happy that she'd remembered the Greek name for her wine.

We carried on eating until neither of us felt like we could move.

"So, did you enjoy?" I asked, already knowing the answer.

"Very much," she said, with a grin spread across her face.

"I'll be back in a minute," I said, "I'm going to go pay."

She sat up and screwed her eyebrows, a reaction I expected.

"Why don't we half it?" she asked.

"My treat. Besides, I should have done this ages ago," I said. "It's not up for debate."

After settling with the waiter, we headed back outside to the scooters. I felt more grateful than ever that I decided to try them today because, with the amount of food we'd just eaten, I doubted we would have made the walk back to camp.

It only took Brannon a couple of minutes to gain confidence on the scooter on the way back. It didn't take long for her to push the accelerator all the way down and go racing off in front of me. I could have caught up in no time, but I hovered a little behind. I could see how much she was enjoying this. I wanted to admire her as she admired the view. In my opinion, it wouldn't have been up for debate. Who had the better view? Her with the ocean, or me with her. But we would never agree.

The breeze, getting lighter the closer we got to camp, lifted her hair and waved it behind her. Her silky locks shone in the sunlight. Her body was balanced perfectly on the speeding scooter. She was floating beside the ocean, effortlessly gorgeous. Every so often, she'd turn to find me with her glowing purple eyes. I'd notice the glittering of her bronze skin and the fullness of her lips as she smiled. A smile that told me this is where she wanted to be.

A smile that assured me that I wanted to be here too. Now. Tomorrow. Forever.

Brannon

I saw the golden sands of the beach and realised we were nearly at camp.

"Asher," I called, and he sped up next to me, "Why did I need my swimming costume?"

"We aren't done yet," he said, with a wink that made my heart pound violently against my chest. "Follow me."

I followed him all the way to the forest. We left the scooters at the end of the brick path, leaving the keys in Asher's rucksack. As soon as we got here, I knew what we would be doing.

This is one of our favourite places. A small lagoon surrounded by towering trees that touch branches over the top of the water, creating a ceiling of leaves with hot sunlight dappling through. The lagoon isn't a turquoise blue like the ocean, nor is it as warm, but the water is still clear and inviting.

This location is unknown to the majority of people that visit camp. They are occupied with the beach and lounging by the pools so that they often don't venture into the forest. It's a shame for them but a good thing for us. We get the lagoon to ourselves.

The water is surrounded by wooden slabs to walk on, and a miniature wooden pier stretches from the edge into the centre, with small boats tied to the wooden poles. I remember Asher bringing me here to go in the boats not long after we had met. I remember how his eyes looked neon blue compared to the darker water and how his hair's tight ringlets became brown compared to his usual light chestnut curls.

I looked to him as he was spreading our towels out and unpacking his bag. Suddenly, the things I remembered became the things I could see right now.

"Is summer fruits okay?" Asher asked as he poured some already made juice into plastic cups.

"Definitely," I said, removing my shorts and top.

He looked at me and smiled. A meaningful smile full of admiration and love.

"You're beautiful," he said.

I felt myself blushing. How is it that he still made me feel this way? I should be used to his smile and compliments.

My hair was in a messy bun but Asher didn't believe in not getting your hair wet in water and I didn't want to deal with the knotted hair later. I removed the hair tie and shook my fingers through my hair.

"Purple, wavy hair. My favourite," Asher said, walking over to me with my cup of juice.

"Thank you," I said. "My favourite is curly brown ringlets."

He held my face in his hands and kissed my lips, soft but with passion.

"Let's get in."

He took my hand and we walked to the edge of the pier, taking a seat and dipping our feet in. Asher shivered.

"Wow, it's cold," he said.

"You'll be fine," I said.

I lifted myself off the pier and lowered my body into the lagoon. That initial moment, when my shoulders sunk into the water, was cold. But as I allowed gravity to pull me under and my hair to soak in the water, I soon warmed up and adjusted to the temperature.

My head popped back up and I saw Asher watching me.

Asher

She submerged her body into the water without a second thought. As if the water, to her, was the safest place on earth. As if it had been waiting for her, like she was a friend returning. She felt comfortable and fearless. Unlike me, who was used to the warmth of the ocean after a day of the scorching sun heating it up.

"I forgot how much of a water girl you are," I said, seeing the droplets of water dripping onto her smiling mouth.

"Are you getting in then?" she asked.

"Brannon, it's freezing. I need your patience," I said, and she laughed.

"It's warm, I promise," she told me.

"No, it's cold. You think it's warm because you're used to the sea in Cornwall," I said.

She splashed me.

"You're not wrong. When I was in Heston, I did a lot of bodyboarding. There's no feeling quite like the icy sea soaking through a wetsuit and freezing your insides. This? This is nothing," she said.

She made it look easy. Keeping herself up in the water.

"You love it, don't you? Being in there?"

"Almost as much as I love you." My heart smiled. "My dad took me swimming when I was a baby. He always believed it to be the most important thing, knowing how to swim. Especially living in Heston, where a bad storm can make the sea a life-threatening thing. He got me my first bodyboard when I was four. I haven't looked back since. It's the most exhilarating feeling. Don't you think? To feel the water carrying the weight of you, and the motion of the wave speeding to shore," she said.

"I love it," I said. "I mean, you can't always rely on the waves here. It's not always windy enough, or the beach is too full of rocks, so it isn't safe. But I took every chance I could to surf."

"My dad took me to Malibu, once. I think if I could live anywhere in the world, it would be there. Simply for the surfing," she said.

"You don't surf as much in Cornwall?" I asked.

"Oh, we surf," she said, her love for the topic gleaming in her eyes. "Me and dad spent a lot of weekends in Newquay, even more in Porthmeor Beach because it was closer to my house. But, as you said, the sea is freezing. Sometimes the waves are too dangerous to surf. It was easier in Malibu. Easier with dad."

Pain struck her eyes. Grief resurfaced in her heart. And in that moment, where she needed my comfort, she drifted away. To the Myst.

Brannon

I hadn't been here in a while. The red and orange sky was the same. The hot, crimson sun half setting behind the still ocean. The white sand on the ground. Nothing to see behind me.

I half expected Juno to be waiting for me because that's the only reason I've been called here recently. But I couldn't see her. I could see a different lady, strolling towards me.

"Hello, Miss Amory," she said, her voice strong. "I'm Helena. Helena Black."

Helena Black had curly brown hair, blue eyes with wrinkles beneath them and thin, pink lips. She was the same height as me and she didn't strike me as a frail, old lady, although I could tell that age was likely the reason she was here.

"Hello, Mrs Black. It's a pleasure to meet you," I said.

Suddenly I forgot how to act. I forgot what to say. I forgot how to be helpful. I hadn't done this in a while. My routine left my mind.

"I understand that you might be feeling scared-"

"Oh, I'm not scared. I know what to expect. I've known it for years. And I've known that, for me, the Myst won't be how it is for some of my friends," Helena interrupted.

"Why not?" I asked. "Mr Curator and I kept the pendants. You can practise magic or vampirism or life as a werewolf."

"I'm a witch, and an unfortunate one at that. I can't practice magic over there. The sky won't allow it," she said.

For a moment, I was confused. But I caught on pretty quickly. "You're a Lunar witch?" I asked.

"And a proud one, too," she said.

I smiled at her pride in who she was. She smiled back, and I sensed that she hadn't expected me to smile in the first place.

"I'm surprised you've heard of us," she said. "No one mentions us anymore. We were forgotten, as soon as the sacrifice was made."

I didn't know what to say. I didn't know enough to say anything, but I thought I better offer something. "I have heard of them. I just found out my best friend shares a blood line with one," I managed, unsure as to why I was telling her this.

She didn't reply straight away.

"If there's one thing I've never questioned in life, it's fate," she said, smiling into the distance. I sensed that she may have felt slightly smug, and I didn't blame her. "Lunar witches haven't been treated fairly. Oh, no. But when power isn't on your side, what else can you do but accept it?"

"I suppose if you were really desperate to change something, then you'd find a way," I said, not believing that accepting is a good enough excuse for not trying.

The smile did not disappear from her face. Rather, it widened. "History knows as well as I do that the Sol ancestors were desperate to keep themselves away from us. Yet, here we are. And there you are, apparently. A Sol witch and a Lunar witch, best friends," she said.

"We've been best friends since birth, pretty much. But he didn't know about the supernatural world until recently. He didn't tell me, either. So we aren't that great of friends right now," I told her.

"It's hard. When friends do that," she said, placing a hand on my upper arm. "But trust me dear, if you had to find out the history of Lunar witches, and then had to accept that you are one compared to your ever-powerful Sol witch best friend? That's even harder."

I paused. I hadn't thought about how much Blain had had to go through recently.

"I don't know enough about them to know if you're right or not. But I get your point," I said.

She removed her hand from my arm. She stared into the distance, the sun reflecting in her eyes.

"If I could give you any advice as a pendant holder, it would be to make yourself aware. Learn about the Sol witches, but also learn about the Lunar witches. Make sure that the impression you have on the witching world is a complete one," she said.

"I'm trying, really hard, to learn about your witching kind. But the few books that we have show no trace of Lunar witches," I said.

She rolled her eyes, disappointment breaking her gaze. She didn't talk for a while. But when she did, the disappointment was pushed aside and anticipation motivated her every word.

"You and your best friend, you aren't talking right now I assume?" she asked.

"No, we're not," I said.

"Well, if you want to learn about the Lunar witches, and if the books aren't helping you to do so, then it looks like you're going to have to start the conversation."

She was right. What other option did I have?

"You strike me as a good person, Miss Amory," she said.

"You can call me Brannon," I said.

"Brannon, you strike me as a confident girl, who knows what she wants, and knows how to get it," she said.

I felt my face turn red at the compliment.

"I've met very few Lunar witches, but every one of them gives me the impression that they aren't treated as equals by the Sol witches," I said, deflecting the conversation from myself. "That doesn't sit right with me."

"I think, maybe, you're the first pendant holder in four centuries to feel that way," she said.

Without meaning to, I felt defensive. My dad was a pendant holder and I know for a fact that he wouldn't have been okay with it.

"I think the problem is that for every generation following Juno's sacrifice, Lunar witches were just not mentioned. Asher's dad is one of the most knowledgeable people I know when it comes to supernatural life, and he knows nothing about you," I said.

She nodded in agreement. "Perhaps you're right," she said.

Now we were both looking into the distance. I snooped around her emotions. She felt satisfied and hopeful. I felt pressure.

"I don't know how to make it right," I said, honestly.

She turned to me and held my hands.

"If it's up to you to make it right, you will. Fate never fails. That's one thing that us witches can agree on," she said, squeezing my hands even tighter. "I think that if it wasn't meant to be you, then you wouldn't be best friends with a Lunar witch. I think you need to talk to him. Learn from him. And then, work with him." She paused. "I think that fate would be stupid to not choose you."

I felt motivation grow within me. Every bone in my body wanted to fix this. Whatever it was that needed fixing.

"Truthfully, I feel like I might fail. But 'might' doesn't satisfy me. I need to know for sure. I won't stop until I've exhausted every method possible to making things right for the Lunar witches," I said.

She smiled, ambitiously. "Sometimes history and fate agree with time," she said. "There's a reason I died at this moment, and there's a reason you were the one to greet me here."

It hit me. She was about to pass away into the afterlife. She wasn't here to help me.

"I'm so sorry, Mrs Black. This shouldn't be about my problems. I should be making this experience easier for you. Helping you find peace," I said, squeezing her hands back.

She looked directly into my eyes. "Brannon Amory, I think you'll be the one to save us all," she said. "I'll hold onto that hope over there." She nodded towards the sun. "That, in itself, is peace."

She let go of my hands and walked off. As soon as she left my side, I felt the absence of her presence. She straightened things out in my mind. Because of her, my path moving forward was clear.

She didn't turn back. She headed straight for the sun. Sadness settled in my throat as the sun swallowed her into its glow.

Rest well, Mrs Helena Black. I swear, I'll do my best.

Asher

She was in the water when her eyes closed and the Myst called her. I suddenly didn't care how cold the water was. It didn't occur to me to care. I jumped straight in, grabbing her arm and pushing her to the surface.

She was light in the water, but it was more difficult to push her onto the pier. I got her upper body on there first, then pushed her legs to lift her higher. Eventually, I got her up, safe and out of the water, but she didn't look comfortable.

I pushed my own body weight out of the water and picked her up in my arms. I laid her down as gently as I could on her towel. Then, I sat beside her and held her hand. I didn't care that I was soaking wet. I didn't care that I was cold or that my arms ached from forcing her out of the lagoon. All I cared about was her, and when she would reopen her gorgeous eyes.

Her episode lasted a while. I wondered whether Juno had summoned her, and why she didn't want me as well. The thought of me also having an episode made me feel sick. Brannon would have drowned. Timing is more powerful than us all.

Her fingers began to move, and her eyelids flickered before opening. Her movement was stiff as she came around. I brushed her hair off her face.

"Are you okay?" I asked her.

Her eyes moved between me and the water. She wouldn't be able to recall me moving her. That was something I would never get used to; not remembering my life whilst I was in the Myst.

She held her hand on her forehead. I leant down and kissed it. She didn't react.

It took her a few minutes to sit up, but when she did, she was adamant about what she needed to do.

"Asher," she said, "I need to talk to Blain."

Brannon

He looked confused. We had been having such a lovely day, with no mention of Blain. But, after conversing with Mrs Black, I felt a sense of desperation. Desperation to change what was going to be her experience in the Myst.

My head was pounding. I hadn't missed this feeling.

"Okay," Asher said. "I can message him. Let's go back first and change. You need to take some tablets, too."

I stood up and started folding my towel. I put my clothes back on over my swimming costume and repacked Asher's bag. He mirrored my fast-paced actions, knowing nothing about what had just happened, but trusting that talking to Blain was the best thing to do.

I put the rucksack on Asher's back before turning him around to face me.

I pressed my lips against his.

"You saved me," I said.

He smiled. He thought that I wouldn't realise but I had sensed his disappointment, even though he wasn't one to beg for appreciation.

We walked back to the scooters, which I had forgotten were there. I was pleased at the sight of them. We would get back quicker. We dropped them off at his house. Asher went inside to get changed and I ran back to my cabin to do the same.

Asher messaged to tell me that Blain had agreed to meet us at the pier at sunset.

I changed into a navy-blue dress and white trainers. Then I waited.

Asher

She hadn't explained the urgency to see Blain, nor what had happened to her in the Myst. But I didn't feel the need to know. I followed her. I'd follow her anywhere.

I told my dad that I didn't need food because Brannon and I had eaten a lot of Greek food already. He wanted to know about the scooters. How fast they went, how reliable they were, were they prone to damage, that sort of thing. Then mum wanted to know what we ate in town and if Brannon enjoyed it. Should she start cooking Greek food when Brannon came round for dinner or was a simple spag bol still okay?

I knew the sun had started to set as beams of light flooded the kitchen with gold. I was trying to wrap up my conversation with my parents in a polite way.

I told them I had to meet Brannon to watch the sunset, which led to more questions about the weather and them telling me to take a jacket in case we're out late.

By this point, Brannon would already be at the pier, eager to start this much needed conversation. It was possible that Blain would be there, too. But actually, what worried me more was that Blain wouldn't be there. He might avoid her again now that she knows the truth. It might just be Brannon, feeling disappointed that she wouldn't get her answers.

Brannon

I laid a picnic blanket on the pier. The wood was too hot to sit on. Then I waited.

The sun settled the eagerness within me. I watched as the lemon-yellow ball of heat slowly descended from the sky, turning into a golden semicircle, painting the sky with shades of pink and purple. Different from the Myst. But equally charming.

Equal. A word I kept repeating to myself. After all, that's what this problem came down to. Equality between the witches. Just because, by the sound of it, our power isn't equal, should that justify unequal treatment? An unequal afterlife?

The answer was no. I knew that wouldn't change for me. But I needed to know everything about the witches, both Sol and Lunar, to decide what I could do next.

As I heard footsteps walking down the pier, I turned around quickly. Blain. The sun shone on his silky black hair as it slicked across his head. He forced a smile, but I could feel his sadness. He was scared.

He walked to me, eyes on the ground. His usual confidence was gone. I hated this.

"Hey, Bran," he said as he sat down cross-legged in front of me.

"Hi, Blain."

He was wearing a baby blue T-shirt and black jean shorts. Around his neck was the crescent necklace.

"Look, Brannon, I-"

"I think it's best we wait until Asher's here."

Blain continued to stare at the ground until Asher arrived. It felt like a long wait. And despite how motivated I felt following my conversation with Mrs Black, I had no idea what to say or where to start.

Asher ran down the pier. My frustration at him being late melted away as he sat beside me. The sun highlighted his turquoise eyes. A perfect colour match to the ocean.

"Sorry, parents would not stop talking," Asher said, with an awkward laugh to follow. "So, where do we start?"

Blain looked at him, sorrow flooding his eyes.

"Guys, I need you to know how sorry I am. You were the first people I wanted to tell. It was so hard for me to keep this from you," Blain said. He looked directly at me. "Leaving the words was the only thing connecting me to you."

I didn't say anything.

"I think the problem was that the words haunted Brannon, and me, for such a long time. It was quite a creepy thing to do," Asher said.

"I know. I didn't intend for it to bother you this much, but I understand why it has," Blain said.

He looked at me, desperately trying to understand how I felt. I didn't have to try very hard to know that he was feeling an abundance of guilt, and I felt how sorry he truly was.

There was a bigger problem to deal with now. I wasn't completely sure what, but I knew that it required me and Blain to be on the same team. And, aside from that, I'd missed him for long enough. I just wanted my best friend back.

"Look," I said, "you hurt me. You upset me and you made me angry. But I would be a hypocrite if I ended our friendship over this. I have lied to you for eighteen years, not being able to tell you that half of me is supernatural. Not being able to tell you that meeting Asher was much more serious than having a holiday romance. Not being able to get your advice about keeping the pendant or not." Suddenly, I was the one feeling guilty. "Blain, I don't blame you for not telling me this. Your nan asked you not to, and I understand that's more important than telling me. But-" I paused to take a breath. "I do blame you for not talking to me for months. I was patient and understanding, but also lonely and lost without you. That's how you hurt me."

Tears welled in Blain's eyes. Asher placed a hand on my knee.

"There's no excuse," Blain said. "I just knew I'd end up telling you if I spoke to you."

And just like that, I understood. I didn't need any more explanations.

"Blain, I forgive you. And I hope you can forgive me too," I said, reaching for his hand.

Without warning, he flung himself at me. His arms swung around my neck, and he buried his face in my shoulder. Then I felt another pair of arms come from behind.

"I love you guys," I heard Blain say, his voice muffled in all the arms.

"That's not the end of the chat, you two," I said, pushing them off but smiling with them. "Blain, I need to know everything you know about the Lunar witches. There's little to no information written down and Juno isn't willing to talk about it. You know who Juno is don't you?"

"Queen of the heavens," Blain said.

"Good. Well, anyway, she won't say much about it. I know that there's some kind of division between the witches and that the Lunar witches got dealt an unfair hand," I said.

"As the pendant holders, we might be able to do something to help," Asher said.

This filled me with happiness. Me and Asher hadn't spoken greatly on my desire to deal with this problem, but he wanted to help without me asking him too.

"Look, I'll tell you what my nan's told me. But there's probably more that she hasn't," Blain said.

Asher

Brannon and I listened to everything Blain had to say.

"My nan has been friends with the Amorys for decades. Our families have always kept in contact due to their witching connections, though they were never majorly close. Brannon, we became best friends naturally. No one forced me. But my nan knew who you were, and she knew why you wore that pendant. She always told me not to ask questions about you fainting. That it's rude to question someone's health. So, I never did. Aside from that, she let us get on with it," Blain explained. "However, even I noticed that when the letter came home about camp, she seemed rather pushy. She told me it was because we wouldn't get a chance like this again, two best friends going to a summer camp together. But she hadn't been like that about any other school trips. Although I sensed something was up, I didn't dig any deeper. It was only recently that I found out she was pushy because she saw the name Curator on the letter. She told me it was fate, that an Amory had been invited to the home of a Curator, weeks before their 18th birthdays. She said that you, Brannon, had to go. There were no two ways about it. I had no idea how significant you two meeting was, or the decision you had to make that day. I had no idea that if you didn't keep the pendants and moved to

Greece, that you wouldn't be able to see each other ever again. I can't imagine how difficult that was to decide."

"It wasn't difficult for me. I didn't care about her surname, I knew she was the one for me," I said, reassuring Blain, in case he had any doubts, that I stayed with Brannon for supernatural reasons.

He smiled, then continued talking. "After camp, when my grandad died, my nan started talking to me about strange things. Like the whereabouts of the witches. Or a place called the Myst that she would go to one day, or how the air felt different since we got home from camp. Well, I thought she was going mad. I thought the death of her husband had sent her over the edge. I told her that she needed to seek help from someone else. That there was no such thing as witches or the Myst. But then, one day, she got rather frustrated with me and said you, Brannon, would understand. That was when I questioned if she was really going mad or if she was telling the truth."

He took a breath. I looked at Brannon. She was okay. He carried on.

"I sat her down one day and told her to explain to me what on earth she was talking about, and she did. She told me that our ancestor was one of the most powerful Lunar witches and that there is magic in our blood. She explained that when either of us die, we will be sent to an afterlife in the Myst, which you both anchor. She explained to me your fainting, your headaches, your pendants, your duties. Anyway, the next day I found out that Asher's family were sick. I told Nan, and she immediately knew this was a consequence of the Myst being alive again. That the amount of power that had built up over time was more than necessary for the Myst to function, so it was trying to find a home in the previous generation of pendant holders." He sighed. "Brannon, she knew straight away that's what killed your dad."

For the first time, Brannon's gaze broke. She looked around. Everywhere but at Blain. I looked into the future. She wasn't going to get upset. Blain would just continue talking.

"At this point, my nan told me about Juno. She told me her official title and that she created the Myst and the pendants. She told me she was the most powerful, well-respected witch to ever exist, and that she would have the solution to this problem. My nan figured that Juno would have to alter the spell that was used to create the Myst, and that the only way to gain enough power to do that was through objects left in the Modern World. Juno told people close to her which objects she would be leaving behind in case she ever needed that much power again, which she highly doubted due to her sacrificing herself. Juno thought she could trust these people, but she shouldn't have. Word spread quickly about the objects and everyone started hunting for them. It took all these centuries for us to collate them all, my nan figuring some of them out herself."

"It's not like the objects were at your house, though. They were in buildings all around Heston," Brannon said, confused.

"My nan didn't want to have the objects in her possession. She just wanted to know where they were, or who had them. She followed their whereabouts her entire life. She felt that was her duty," Blain said.

"And you made sure they were in their rightful place or with the right person before you left the note and disappeared," Brannon said.

"Yes. It wasn't always easy. I had to dig up a sign post for those rings. Do I look like someone who should be digging?" Blain asked, making light of the situation.

Brannon laughed. "Okay, I understand that bit. What happened when I had all the objects and returned to Asher?" she asked.

"We waited. Then, when you messaged me to tell me that Asher's family were better, we knew that the spell had been done," Blain said.

"Did your nan tell you why she wanted to help Brannon find the objects?" I asked.

"Well, to begin with, she told me that Juno made the ancestors with the objects swear a magical oath to never move locations. She knew the objects were around Heston, but she wanted to make it easier for Brannon by making sure that Juno's notepad would direct her correctly. Then she told me that she wanted to help because she wanted the spell to be altered. She said that it would be highly likely that Juno would have to give you two the excess power of the Myst, granting you with powers of your own." Me and Brannon shot each other a look. Blain didn't know if this had happened, yet. "She said that if you both had powers then you would have more of a say over the Myst in general. Your involvement meant that people had to listen to you. You wouldn't just be the anchors anymore. You'd be connected to the Myst, have its power running in your veins."

"What did she want to change about the Myst?" Brannon asked.

"She didn't tell me and, to be honest, I didn't ask. At this point, I was fed up. Fed up with finding objects, fed up with leaving words, fed up with lying for her. I told her that she should be honest and talk to you, that's the only way to get anything done. But she wanted to give you time to adjust to a new life. She said that it was unlikely that you'd want to help her."

"I do want to help her," Brannon said.

"I know," Blain replied.

"So, to summarise," I said, "your nan wants to change something about the Myst for the Lunar witches before she dies."

"To put it in simple and very blunt terms, yes," Blain said.

"Well, we need to find out what she wants to change," Brannon said.

We all agreed. Silvia, Blain's nan, was clearly desperate to alter something that Juno had done. I don't believe that she would have put Brannon and Blain through this if it wasn't important.

"Okay," Blain said, "my turn to ask questions."

"Fire away," Brannon said.

"Did you know Asher was a Curator?" Blain asked.

"No. My dad didn't read the letter and my mum didn't know that the surname meant anything. We don't tell her or Marley anything about magic or supernatural life. They don't need to know," Brannon said.

"That's what my family decided for me, too," Blain said.

Brannon

His words paused in bold letters in my brain. I briefly questioned whether keeping them, Blain, my mum, Marley, from the depths of this life was a good thing, or if it was just easier. For a moment, I questioned whether it should be their choice to know or not.

"When did you realise who the other person was?" Blain asked.

"Brannon noticed my pendant in the pictures taken at the bonfire. I knew as soon as I saw her. Her purple hair and eyes gave it away," Asher said.

"Did you tell each other as soon as you realised?" Blain asked.

"No. We were both scared to say it. Then I had an episode on the mountain hike. I think that said it all for us," I answered.

"This one's important," Blain said. "Asher, what was your first opinion on me?"

We both laughed. A sense of normality returned as Blain was finally being his old self again.

"I remember hoping that you were related so that I had no competition. You can imagine how overjoyed I was to find out you were gay," Asher said.

"And you can imagine how disappointed I was to find out you were straight," Blain replied, and we all broke off into fits of laughter.

"Is that question time over?" Asher asked.

"I have one more," Blain said. "Is it true? Do you really have powers?" His voice was now serious. He was intrigued.

Asher and I smiled and nodded. This was the only information that neither we nor Blain could fully get our heads around.

"I can read people's emotions," I said. "And Asher can see a short while into the future. They aren't overly impressive powers. They aren't dangerous."

"Juno told us that the power would get to know us. Brannon is a very emotionally intelligent person, so her powers surround emotions. I am extremely bad at not knowing, so my powers surround the future," Asher explained.

"Will they get stronger?" Blain asked.

This was something that I had asked myself but never asked out loud.

"We haven't had these powers for very long. I think the power from the Myst is still finding a home in us, and the more it does so, the more advanced the powers will get. For example, Brannon might be able to read minds, one day. And I, eventually, might be able to see weeks or months ahead of time," Asher said.

"That's crazy. I mean, you're the only two witches alive with power," Blain said.

"It's not as great as it sounds," I said, surprising both Blain and Asher. "There's no one alive to teach us how to use them. Sometimes I wish we could venture into the Myst, way past the borderline, and get some magic lessons."

"You can't go into the Myst?" Blain asked.

"Nope. Just to the doorway," I said.

"Still," Blain said, "you're witches. That's quite something."

We smiled in agreement.

"It's weird though, isn't it?" Blain continued. "There's two types of witches and two pendants, yet the pendants both belong to Sol descendants. No wonder no one knows about the Lunar witches."

Asher

As soon as he said it, Brannon's eyes widened dramatically.

"Blain," she said, "I think you just hit the nail on the head."

She stood up and started to yank the picnic blanket from underneath Blain and I. We scrambled to our feet before being flipped like pancakes.

She'd figured something out. Or Blain had, and she had an idea of what to do. But the sun had nearly set, and this was no time to become a hero.

"Brannon, it's late gorgeous," I said, taking her hand.

"But-"

"There's nothing you can do to change anything tonight," I said.

"Brannon, I think the next step is to talk to my nan. She knows much more than she's told me," Blain said.

"Blain's right," I agreed.

She dropped her shoulders and the urgency to solve the problem reduced.

"Okay," she said, sitting back down on the edge of the pier.

We sat either side of her. Blain took one of her hands.

"I've missed your go-getter attitude," he said.

She smiled, gripping his hand.

I took her other hand.

"It's hard to keep up with," I said, and Blain laughed.

"That's why we love you," he told her.

She planted a kiss on each of our cheeks. Everything wasn't fine. But it was okay, just for one moment, to pretend that it was.

Brannon's eyes examined the sky. Mine and Blain's followed.

What a rare sight. The edge of the sun peaked over the horizon, an orange and crimson glow on the bottom half of the sky. A little bit higher up, the silver moon positioned itself for night-time. It wasn't quite full, but it dazzled brilliantly still.

And I wondered how often this happened. How often two opposing creations of nature could be seen in the same sky, with no attempt to outshine the other, just simply uniting as partners.

Brannon

For the first time in a while, I slept undisturbed. I knew who had left the words. I had made up with my best friend. I had decided my next move. Life felt a little clearer. Even if it was also a little more extraordinary.

Unbeknown to Asher, these situations made me thrive.

I could of course sit on a beach, tanning in the sunshine, cooling off from the heat with a dip in the sea. I could drink a fruity lemonade and watch the sunset before having an evening walk by the ocean. I could live a wonderful life here, feeling grateful for everything I'm lucky enough to call mine. I could feel happy in a normal life.

Before Asher, I would have considered it the only option for me. A normal girl with a normal life.

But I don't think I want that anymore. Not when I could explore the witching world, learn the spells and allow my power to grow. Not when I could embrace my ability to help the supernatural community find peace after death. Not when I could discover what it is that deeply hurts the Lunar witches and take the opportunity to fix things.

I knew that I wouldn't be able to rest, now. Not until I had answers. Not until I had a solution.

Blain told me he would arrange a time for me to talk to his nan. He said it shouldn't take long to persuade her to open up. After all, she wanted this more than anyone else.

I received a message from him in the early afternoon. Asher and I had been replacing the fairy lights on the fence in my garden with some light bulb shaped ones. I was determined to make my garden summer fit and figured it would be a good distraction.

"What did he say?" Asher asked when my phone pinged.

"To meet him and his nan later on, by the old bonfire."

"Sharing witchy knowledge around a fire in the dark? Sounds fitting."

"I'm going to struggle to wait that long."

"It's fine. We will sort out some more bits in your garden. Then we'll need to change into warmer clothes, grab a blanket and some chairs, because I dread to think how uncomfortable that tree trunk will be, and we'll head down there to start the fire," Asher said.

"Will Silvia be able to walk through the woods to the bonfire?" I asked, not recalling if the path was safe.

"Yes. It's not a very long walk and the path was recently cleared of larger rocks and sticks. Blain will be with her, and she doesn't come across as unable," he said.

I nodded before continuing to hang the new lights on hooks. "What else do we need to do?" I asked.

"I need to check the chlorine levels in your pool, so we'll walk to mine to get some chlorine tablets."

"Okay," I said, "Let's go."

Asher

As we walked back to mine, we said hello to the new holiday arrivals from this morning's flight. When we got to my house, my parents were in the garden, sunbathing.

"Hello, you two," my mum said, smiling as always.

"What are you after?" my dad asked.

"Chlorine tablets," I said.

"In the shed. We've just done our pool, actually, so I know there's a few left," he said.

As I went off to the shed, Brannon took a seat next to my mum.

"What's your plans for the rest of the day?" I heard mum ask.

"We're going to sort my pool out and work on my garden a little bit. Then we have plans with Blain and his nan," Brannon told her.

"The bonfire's free tonight, isn't it, Dad?" I asked, returning to take a seat, tablets in hand.

"Yep, I'll make a note that you'll be using it," he said.

"We're meeting his nan to talk about the Lunar witches," Brannon said.

I hadn't intended telling my parents this part, but I knew Brannon wanted to.

"What are you hoping to gain from it?" my dad asked.

"I want to know what happened to the Lunar witches. And why they're so unhappy with the way things are," Brannon said.

My dad looked concerned. "Do you think it's worth it? I mean, even if you know, what difference will it make?"

"I might not be able to do anything," Brannon said, a sense of defensiveness in her tone, "but I might as well try. And, anyway, wouldn't you like to know what happened all those years ago?"

My dad smiled. "Yes, I would," he said. "Fair enough, fair enough. I hope you get what you want out of it. But, Brannon, I feel it's my responsibility to tell you that witches are complicated. Don't go setting yourself impossible tasks."

Brannon smiled, but it wasn't her usual broad and happy grin. It seemed to me to be her way of saying thank you for the advice but don't doubt me like that. She excused herself to go to the toilet.

"You forget, Roger, that she saved your life," my mum said, shaking her head at my dad.

"I didn't forget, Tam. I just don't want her to convince herself that this will be an easy thing to do," he said.

I was the one feeling defensive now.

"She doesn't think that," I said.

"Roger, she packed up her life and moved country. If she hadn't done that, we would have lost our son. Then she went on a magical mission for the most important woman in witching history to save you and your mother. And don't forget that, every day, she loves our son so very much," my mum said, verbalising my thoughts.

"Tammy, I know! I think the world of her, you know I do."

"Then it wouldn't hurt to show some encouragement."

I stayed quiet and they said nothing more, but I knew Mum was disappointed in Dad. I also knew that Dad felt guilty for doubting Brannon.

When Brannon came back outside, we decided it was time to leave.

"Did he upset you?" I asked as we walked back.

"Your dad? No, why?" she said.

"You walked off," I said.

"I went to the toilet," she said.

"You didn't even go in the bathroom," I said.

She shot me a look. One of her looks that tells me she's figured out what I've done.

"You looked into the future?" she asked.

"Only to see if you were upset. And you were," I said, honestly.

"Okay," she said. "I was upset. But only because I'd used my powers, too."

"Why?"

"I wanted to know how your dad felt. I couldn't figure out if he was giving me genuine advice or if he just had no belief in me."

"And?" I asked.

"And I got upset because I saw that, really, he just cares about me a lot and doesn't want me to feel like a failure," she said. "He's the closest thing I have to a fatherly figure now. It made me emotional to know he cares."

I squeezed her hand. Nothing else needed to be said.

We went back to Brannon's garden. She got us pink lemonade whilst I worked on the pool, correcting the chlorine levels and checking that the lights worked. We mowed the lawn, watered the flowers that she had planted, cleaned her garden furniture and continued to position the decorations she had brought. By the end of the day, which came around fast, her garden was a palette of green, blue, pink and white. The grass was cut into perfect strips, the pool was ready, the flowers blooming, and the fence lit up with lights. She loved it. So did I.

When the sun had half set, we changed into jumpers and grabbed a couple of blankets and chairs before heading down to the woods. Setting out the chairs, we lit the fire and waited.

Brannon

The flames from the bonfire jumped frantically. Their burnt orange glow stretched for the night sky, falling back down as their reach proved too ambitious.

The smell of burning wood forced me to reminisce on the day I met Asher. It was déjà vu at its finest.

Blain and Silvia's footsteps could be heard over the crackling of the wood, and the blurred edges of their faces could be seen through the tangerine fire, as it spat and sprinkled crimson hot droplets on the floor. Like a deathly rain fall.

"Hi, Silvia," I said, in as friendly a tone as I could muster, trying to kick us off on the right foot.

Blain gave me a quick hug before sitting down.

"This feels very formal," Blain said.

"Don't be silly, it's a bonfire," Silvia said. "Let's cut to the chase. Brannon."

I looked directly at Silvia. She might have been about to tell me that I couldn't do this. Or that I overreacted by walking off. Or that this isn't my place to get involved. But my only aim was to show her how serious I was about this, and how badly I wanted to help.

"I want to apologise," Silvia said, unexpectedly. She was here to answer my questions, not apologise to me. "I've given it some thought and I don't think I dealt with this in the best way possible. Unfortunately, age does not mean you don't make mistakes. And I would like you to forgive me for mine."

I hadn't realised how much I needed to hear this. The relief flooded through me. "Thank you, Silvia. Yes, I forgive you, I forgive Blain, I forgive it all. I kept secrets, too," I said.

"That's very kind of you. Thank you," Silvia said. "So, tell me why you wanted to talk to me."

I was reminded of her kindness, and how welcoming she could be. The Silvia I remembered. "Okay, well, I've spoken to a few Lunar witches now. At the time, I was unaware of them. But after finding the objects, specifically the rings, it was clear to me that there were two types of witches, and after interacting with some of them myself, it was clear that there's a divide. Firstly, I want to know what caused the divide. And secondly, I want to know what I can do as a pendant holder, and now a home to the power of the Myst, to bring equality to the witches. I don't know what it is, but I know that not everyone is as excited for a magical afterlife as others," I said.

She smiled. A thankful, genuine smile. "You, a Sol witch, wants to help us?" she asked.

"Of course we do," Asher said. "We have the power to at least have a say. Juno has to hear us out. What type of people would we be if we didn't try?"

I noticed a tear leaking from Silvia's eyes. This meant more to her than I had first thought.

"This story starts before the Myst was in discussion. It may take me a while to explain," Silvia said.

Asher

Fireflies circled the tips of the flames. The sky was clear, and the stars were shyly twinkling, like a hushed audience, not wishing to shine too brightly.. There was a cold breeze, but we had covered our legs in blankets, and the heat from the fire was enough to keep us warm. The full sphere of the silver dusted moon hovered above us, and Silvia began her story.

"It's common knowledge that witches are known to be nature's servants. But the witching community comes hand in hand with a superiority complex." Silvia's dark eyes were lit up by the flames. "The witches got their magic from the Earth, and the Earth is circled by the sun and the moon, which is why the witches guess they were divided between the two. But it is also common knowledge that the sun is bigger than the moon. And, therefore, magic mirrored that. The Sol witches were more powerful. The only time the witches had an equal amount of power was on a night like this one."

She looked at the sky and we all followed her gaze. "A full moon."

Silvia's words, her voice, the fire, the forest and the growing darkness, all bathed by the silver light, caused an eerie atmosphere. I could tell by the look on Brannon's face that she was completely fixated.

"So, once a month we would have been as powerful as them?" Blain asked his nan.

She nodded before continuing. "For as long as witches have existed, Juno's family have been the most powerful. They could always do things that the other witches could not."

It became apparent to me that Silvia was probably unaware that Juno was an Amory. I remember Juno telling us that people didn't relate her to the Amory ancestor because she was a bad person. I didn't feel it was the right moment to say anything, so I let her carry on.

"There wasn't a division between the witches for a long time. The Lunar witches accepted that they were less powerful, and they looked forward to that one day a month that they could show off as equals. Everything was, mostly, fine. Until Juno was born.

"Juno's mother was a Lunar witch, and her father was a Sol witch. Her father, wanting his daughter to be as powerful as himself, made Juno choose Sol power. You couldn't have both.

"Juno's father, in desperation for his daughter to be powerful, portrayed the Lunar Witches as weak and worthless. This upset them and that's when the unrest began.

"When Juno was old enough to be the leading Ancestor, she had to take over a divided community of witches that her father made no effort of reuniting for eighteen years. Juno didn't believe her father's opinion on the Lunar witches to be true and she spent ten years working hard to unite the community. She continued to meet up with Ancestor Selene Crescent, head of the Lunar witches. Together, they managed to build a good relationship. After those years, the Lunar witches felt welcome again. Things never really went back to normal, but they were civil, and the Lunar witches showed up to community events and meetings like before.

"The peace lasted for a couple more decades. Earth's magic ran out, and Juno allocated the pendants to the Amory and Curator ancestors, the strongest two below her, to look after the remaining magic. With everyone's powers combined, this added up to a lot. However, when the Amory ancestor started misusing her magic in an uncontrollable and dangerous way, Juno saw no choice but to be rid of magic in the living world. The Curator ancestor was madly in love with the Amory ancestor. He wasn't prepared to stop her. But the Lunar witches thought there was another choice.

"They suggested a pendant be designated to one of them. To Selene. Juno disagreed. She said it was impossible to stop the Amory ancestor, and the only way to do it was to get rid of magic. She was adamant.

"The Myst and the sacrifice was discussed around the community; some witches were in disbelief that Juno would give up her life to create a supernatural afterlife. But it required every ounce of power that Juno could get. It would inevitably take her life, and many others. The death of witches would create an abundance of power in the Old World.

"The Lunar witches didn't want this. They wanted to look for another way. The thing is, they only got to use magic once a month and, in my opinion, it made them appreciate it more than the Sol witches who had access to it every day. The Lunar witches didn't want magic to be a thing of the past. But the Sol witches had their minds made up.

"Juno's most loyal followers, the powerful Ancestors, agreed to the sacrifice. The spell required a lot of power. An unimaginable amount. Juno told Selene and the Lunar witches that the power needed was beyond imagination and so, because the Lunar witches did not want it to happen, they refused to attend, thinking that they could stop it. But Juno had lied. The

Sol magic was more than enough to make the Myst happen. The simple fact was that as a result of their absence, the Lunar witches had no say in the Myst, or the happenings of it in the afterlife. To put it simply, they would forever pass into the Myst due to their supernatural blood, but they would not be able to practice magic like everyone else."

Silvia took a deep breath. Talking about it saddened her.

"Ancestor Selene Crescent discovered the truth and tried to make amends. She tried her hardest to convince the Lunar witches of what was happening and that they should participate in the sacrifice. She believed a better life awaited them in death. But they refused. So, Selene took herself to the location of the sacrifice, and gave up her life like Juno and the others. She was the only Lunar witch to do this. She believed that if she didn't, the Lunar witches would be totally forgotten. They would never again have the chance to practice the spells they love or the rituals they waited monthly for.

"It's unknown whether her interference made a difference. But her courage has been admired ever since. I just hope that she didn't sacrifice herself for nothing."

Brannon

The witching world wasn't totally different to the real world for humans. It was corrupt. It was unequal. It was divided and conquered by power.

"Silvia, I hate to tell you this but the Lunar witches that I have met when anchoring the Myst have not looked forward to their passing. I think the reason Juno won't talk to me about them is because she's ashamed. I don't think Selene's sacrifice made a difference," I said.

"Well, that's why I am doing this," Silvia said. "I am a descendant of Selene Crescent. I owe it to my family that came before me and for those that follow me, to continue what she started."

Asher looked like he was about to burst. "Brannon, tell her," he said.

I knew what he meant. "Okay," I said. "I descended from Juno."

"That can't be possible," Silvia said.

"She told me. She's an Amory. She and her father were always referred to as the leading Ancestors, so no one knew. Then Juno became known as Queen of the Heavens. The bad ancestor, the Amory ancestor, was her little sister. That's probably why she wanted to give up magic. She couldn't have her family go down in history like that," I said.

"I can't believe it," Silvia said. The old lady sat back, a frown so deep I could see it easily in the light of the fire and the moon. Eventually she said, "But it's a good thing."

"How so?" Blain asked.

"Because she will listen to you, Brannon. The leading Ancestor's always deemed family the most important thing," Silvia said, full of hope now.

"I need to find out where the Lunar witches stand in the Myst. Then I'll do all I can to make sure they get the same rights as the Sol witches," I said.

Silvia grinned and rubbed her hands together. "Well, that's enough of the serious talk," she said. "Did anyone bring marshmallows?"

Asher

We spent the evening talking about the time Brannon and Blain hadn't spoken. The things Brannon and I had done in Heston, Silvia interjecting with stories of her teenage days, including infamously getting drunk on the beach in the freezing temperatures of a long-ago January. Our experiences with Juno. Brannon's dad's funeral. Blain's grandad's funeral. Their journey out here. What they thought of camp. It was a beautiful evening spent in the silver light of a full moon and the company of friends.

After the late night, Brannon and I slept in till mid-morning. When we woke up, she felt it important to relay the information we got from Silvia to my dad.

It took an hour or so explaining what we now knew. He was shocked and amazed, intrigued and weary. He found it fascinating but concerning that this information was unknown to supernatural beings in the Modern World.

Brannon told him her next move was to talk to Juno about the lives of the Lunar witches in the Myst.

"It seems like a messy situation," he said to her. "Are you sure you want to get involved? You could be widely hated for it."

"I'm an Amory. I'm used to it," was her response, and that was the end of that conversation.

We spent the day with my parents, sunbathing in the garden, chilling on inflatable donuts and floats in the pool, having a BBQ and then warming up in the hot tub as the sun went down and the heat gradually dissipated.

Brannon tried to sleep but she couldn't. It was nothing to do with my bed, just the fact that her mind was eager to talk to Juno, and she wouldn't rest until it was done.

I agreed to come with her. I was tired but I didn't want her to have to do this herself.

"I'll see you on the other side," I said before we linked hands and closed our eyes.

The last thing I saw was her smile. The smile that made me fall in love over and over again. Then we drifted away. To somewhere only we know.

Brannon

If there's one thing I'm always confident about, it's what to expect when we enter the borderline of the Myst. It never changes. It's continuity.

I clutched my pendant, gently, feeling grateful that I could come here.

Our intentions were understood quickly and, in no time at all, the hooded figure that was Juno was walking towards us, through the perfectly still ocean.

She looked up and removed her hood. Her grey hair looked healthier than ever, and her silver eyes sparkled. Her presence was intimidating. But that hadn't stopped me before.

A toothless smile appeared on her face. She nodded to us in turn.

"Mr Curator. Miss Amory. To what do I owe the pleasure?"

"I'd like to know about the Lunar witches, please, Juno," I said.

I sensed immediately an overwhelming flood of unease pour from Asher. Was it my bluntness? Probably. But I couldn't and didn't want to conjure up small talk. It was pointless. I wanted answers.

Juno tried hard to force her smile, but it was obviously fake. She wanted to turn around and pretend I hadn't said anything, or so I guessed. I had to guess, because I couldn't feel her emotions. As hard as I tried, there was nothing. Perhaps she was too strong for my minor powers to compete with.

"Very well," she said, her smoky eyes piercing through mine. "What is it that you'd like to know?"

"What's it like for them in the Myst?" I asked.

She inhaled sharply. I didn't need powers to sense how uncomfortable she felt. How desperately she didn't want to answer my questions.

"And, Miss Amory, would you kindly inform me of why this is of interest to you?"

"Of course. I've been interested in the witches since I found the rings. There was obviously a clear distinction between two types of witches. And then I remembered how some witches who passed through here were not looking forward to their experience in the Myst. I remember one telling me that it isn't the same for everyone. And, if that's true, it needs changing," I said.

Juno took a moment, taking in everything I had said. I knew it was likely that no one had questioned the status-quo in four hundred years. I wasn't surprised to see that she was shocked.

"Miss Amory, the truth is that, no, it isn't the same for everyone."

"What's different?" Asher asked from beside me.

"It's a long story, I'm afraid," Juno said.

I felt a sudden anger surge inside me. She wasn't going to tell us. She was going to try to deflect all my questions. "Don't worry, Juno," I said. "We don't need you to explain what was done. We know that story. It was explained to us by Silvia Crescent. I want to know what difference it makes."

I knew it. I knew it as soon as I saw how her face dropped. She couldn't pretend or avoid anymore. The surname Crescent told her that we knew the truth and that we'd learnt it from a Lunar witch. Juno held her hands together, tightly.

"Very well. I'm assuming you know that the leading Lunar ancestor, Selene Crescent, sacrificed herself with me and the Sol ancestors?" she asked.

We nodded.

"Her sacrifice interfered with the creation of the Myst." She paused, hesitating to tell us more.

"So, if she managed to interfere, why is it not the same for all witches?" I asked, feeling like I was having to drag the information out of her.

"To put it simply, her sacrifice wasn't useful. There was a hundred Sol witches versus one Lunar witch. She failed to interfere enough," she said.

"So what is different for the Lunar witches?" Asher asked, mirroring my frustration at how difficult these answers were to get.

"In the Old World, four centuries ago, the Lunar witches could only perform magic on a full moon." Juno paused and half turned, raising her arm to the horizon and the perfectly balanced, never changing, half sunset glowing at the edge of the Myst's ocean. "There is never a full moon in the Myst."

Asher

"What?!" Brannon exclaimed. "The Lunar witches don't get to experience their own magic in an afterlife created for the purpose of using magic?"

Juno looked at the ground. Whether it was shame, embarrassment or a dislike to Brannon's anger, I couldn't tell. But I hoped it was shame.

"Miss Amory, the Lunar witches were given the chance to join us in the sacrifice," Juno said, as if that would make it better in Brannon's mind.

"That's not true. They didn't want the Myst and so they thought that by withholding their power they could stop it. You didn't tell them the whole truth. And anyway, what you are saying is that their punishment for refusing to kill themselves is to never have magic again? Despite the fact that the solar witches, who had more power anyway, can use it all the time in the Myst," Brannon said.

"Correct," Juno said. Her one word answer pushed Brannon over the edge.

"How can you be okay with that?" Brannon asked, her eyebrows scrunched in frustration.

There was a long drawn out pause. I felt like we were as suspended as the sunset.

"If I am to be honest, Miss Amory, I am not," Juno finally said.

Brannon glared at her. "Why haven't you done something about it, then?"

"The Myst is a happy place, Miss Amo—"

"Yes, I'm sure it is. For you," Brannon interjected.

Juno had never experienced someone disagreeing so strongly with her before. The shock on her face was almost amusing.

"Miss Amory, please, let me explain. The people in the Myst are happy."

"Have you asked a Lunar witch, then? Do you have proof of that?" Brannon asked.

"The Lunar witches," Juno looked to the ground. This time the sadness in her eyes was all too evident. "They do not converse with me."

Brannon did not answer immediately. Although she was fuming with Juno, Brannon's weakness was the emotional vulnerability of others. She struggled to see anyone feel sad.

"Then it's unfair of you to say that the people in the Myst are happy," Brannon said, lowering her voice and softening her tone.

"Yes, I understand," Juno said.

"Juno, I heard you say that Ancestor Crescent's sacrifice did have some interference, despite it not being enough. What was that?" I asked.

Juno looked up at me, briefly looking to Brannon first, who was staring into the distance, rage still burning in her eyes. She could have set fire to the sun, I thought, with a glare so passionate.

"Ancestor Crescent's presence meant that she became a sort of a veto. Or perhaps a casting vote would be a better description. Anything that happens to the Myst has to be approved of by herself, and if she doesn't approve, we need to use overwhelming force," she said.

Brannon's glare had turned to a frown. I felt my own face mirroring hers. "What do you mean?" I asked.

"Let me give you some examples. Firstly, the sun over the sea is half set. Or perhaps half risen. It is fixed and so it cannot dominate the sky because the Myst was not only created by solar witches.

"Additionally, you may happen to remember, when I performed the spell to remove the excess power from your father and grandmother to place it in the pendant holders, being the both of you, the sun, for the only time in the Myst, fell from the sky."

"Everything went dark. I saw a ball of silver shoot across the sky. I said to myself that it looked like a moon," Brannon said, continuing to stare at the sun.

"Correct, Miss Amory. That was Selene, refusing my permission," Juno said.

"Why was she refusing it?" I asked.

"She refused because she did not agree with giving powers to members of the Modern World," Juno said.

"But your spell worked?" I asked.

"Yes, Mr Curator. Because there is far more Sol power than Lunar power. It took some effort, but I overpowered Selene," Juno said.

We all stood in silence for a moment. Processing. Questioning. Wondering.

"So, if the magic behind the Myst was altered in the way we believe it should be, Ancestor Selene would need to give her permission?" I asked.

"Which wouldn't be a problem," Brannon said, moving her gaze to Juno, "because she would agree that this has to be done."

Juno said nothing, her head down.

"Juno, you must agree that it has to be done? It's not fair. The Lunar witches are being discriminated against, and punished, for something that happened four hundred years ago," Brannon continued. "Everyone should have access to their powers in an afterlife that promises that."

Juno raised her head. Her face had changed, subtly. She looked more like her old self. More resolute. "No, I'm afraid there's nothing I can do," she said.

"Why?" Brannon asked.

"I cannot keep changing the Myst. It was made this way for a reason—"

"Yes, to punish the Lunar witches," Brannon interrupted. This time the interruption did not stop Juno.

"Some things cannot be changed. There is simply no—"

"But you found a way to save Asher's family, we can find a way to fix this," Brannon said.

"Miss Amory, I have had enough," Juno said, in a firm and serious voice. "I shall not fix what is not broken. I'm asking you to respect that. Please."

Brannon shook her head. "No, I won't."

Juno exhaled slowly. "Miss Amory, you do remind me so much of my younger self. My father caused unrest between the witches, and I united us again. I understand your desire. But it's just not possible."

Brannon shook her head. That she reminded Juno of her younger self would have once made her feel a sense of pride and accomplishment. This time it meant nothing.

"It was a pleasure to see you both. Truly," Juno said.

I nodded. Brannon stared.

"I hope to hear from you soon and, as ever, I thank you both for the roles you play. They are deeply appreciated," Juno said, pulling her hood over her head and glancing at Brannon one last time before walking into the sunset.

Brannon said nothing. She shut her eyes and returned to the real world. And, as ever, I followed.

Brannon

Our eyes opened and I released Asher's hand.

"I'm going to see Silvia," I said, standing up and almost losing my balance.

"Brannon, it's too late to wake up Silvia," Asher said.

He was right. But what else could I do? Juno was supposed to be my solution. Instead, she was a let-down. She knew the unfairness of the afterlife for the Lunar witches. She understood why it was wrong. But she didn't care. Blood might make us related but she did not resemble me or my family. Because we care. And I act.

The disappointment was dominating. It was painful, even. My hopes were so high for the almighty and powerful Juno to get on board with my plan. To develop my plan into our plan. To do something. Anything.

I felt lost.

"Let's go back to mine," Asher said, intertwining our hands. "Get some sleep, yeah?"

I wouldn't sleep. But I went with him anyway.

We tip toed up the stairs to his room, conscious of a sleeping household. We changed into pyjamas and got into bed. Asher curled himself around me, holding me close . He buried his face in my tangled hair and yawned.

I laid on my back. Arms by my side. Staring at the white ceiling.

"Shut your eyes, Bran. It's been a long day."

His voice was gentle and full of love. I wanted to listen. I wanted to do as he was saying. But I couldn't. I couldn't rest.

Asher

I woke up alone in the bed. Only the lingering scent of Brannon, subtle hints of coconut and mango, told me that she had been here. I hadn't imagined it.

It was midmorning. The sunlight was leaking through my blinds, warming up my bedroom.

I felt tired. My body was well rested, but my mind was far from it.

My parents would be at work. Mum in the camp kitchen offering her help to the chefs for the lunch time buffet. Dad somewhere doing paperwork. The knock at the door was my cue to get out of bed. No one else was here to answer it.

The front of my house was mostly glass which meant I saw Brannon standing there as I ran down the stairs.

I opened the door. Her bronze skin was glowing. Her purple eyes were gentle and not angry. Her lips created a gorgeous smile. Her hair held perfectly in waves.

"Good morning, pretty," I said.

She brought her hands from behind her back and held out a tin-foiled covered plate.

"For you," she said. "I'm sorry for my anger last night."

I wondered when she would learn that I didn't need apologies.

I took the offering and leant in to kiss her cheek.

She followed me to the kitchen, where I opened my gift to reveal rolled up pancakes with sugar sprinkled on top and shortbread biscuits complete with pink icing.

"Wow," I said. "This looks amazing."

She smiled as we tucked in, demolishing the lot.

She thumbed away some icing from the side of my mouth and giggled. I laughed back.

"So, you're feeling better?" I asked.

"I'm feeling less defeated."

"What's today's plan?"

"I messaged Blain. We're going to his cabin, to talk to him and Silvia," she said, which I had guessed would be the answer.

"I mean, you don't have to come. I just assumed you'd want to."

I took her hands in mine. "We're in this together. Of course I'm coming with you," I said and received the most loving grin in reply.

While I got showered and dressed she insisted on cleaning the kitchen counter that we had eaten from. Then we left for Blain's.

Blain led the way to the garden of his cabin. I guess he'd been expecting us as there were four glasses of iced water on the table. Silvia was already out there, sitting forward in one of the wicker chairs, waiting with an eagerness that I'd seen in Brannon many times before.

But Silvia's eagerness was deflated by one look into Brannon's eyes. It was clear that we were the bearers of bad news.

"She won't change it," Brannon said. "She knows how unfair it is. She understands it all. But she won't do anything about it."

Silvia reflected our disappointment. Her voice was flat as she asked quietly, "Why not?"

"She said she won't fix something that isn't broken," I said.

"She wouldn't even entertain the idea," Brannon said.

Blain looked confused. "It makes no sense," he said.

"We found out that Lunar witches do not get to practice magic in the Myst," I said. "There's never a full moon. The speculations, sadly, were true."

Brannon stiffened in her chair as a single tear drop threatened to fall hopelessly from Silvia's eye.

"I tried. I really did," Brannon said, automatically blaming herself.

"I'm sure you did, dear," Silvia said, reassuringly

"She's scared. I know she is," Brannon said. "She doesn't want to upset the Sol witches who are happy with the way things are."

"We know it's not good enough. We don't know what else to do," I said, also feeling like this was my responsibility.

Silvia sipped her water and composed herself. Blain stroked her hand on the table, comforting her. Then, with no further words, she stood up and walked inside.

"I apologise on her behalf," Blain said. "That was a dramatic exit."

Brannon unwillingly giggled. Blain had the ability to make her laugh in moments that I wouldn't even attempt to try.

"I don't blame her," Brannon said. "If I could walk away from this, I would."

"You can," Blain said, now taking Brannon's hand. "This doesn't have to be your problem. You've tried."

"It is my problem. I don't want to anchor a place full of inequality and unfair treatment. It will never sit right with me. And I want to feel proud of my connection to the supernatural, not ashamed," Brannon said. "So, really, I don't blame your nan for walking away."

"I'm not walking away." Silvia reappeared in the doorway, with a wooden, A4-sized box in her hand. It looked ancient and was carved with geometric patterns.

She placed it on the table and looked between myself and Brannon.

"This is for you," Silvia said, pushing the box to us, but more towards Brannon.

She didn't open the lid immediately.

"What is it?"

Silvia simply inclined her head towards the box. Brannon eased the lid off. Inside were a stack of thin sheets of old paper, coloured to a sepia brown and with crinkled edges. Most were laid flat, but some were folded into small squares. I realised there were hundreds of them.

"Letters?" I asked.

"Letters sent by witches, collected by Selene Crescent. She was a very intelligent witch. I suspect that she knew they may have been useful one day," Silvia said.

"What do you want me to do with them?" Brannon asked.

"Nothing," Silvia said, "other than to read them. You might find something. If Juno isn't going to do something about it, maybe we can."

Brannon smiled. Her optimism and go-getter attitude were replicated in Blain's nan.

"I'll read through them. I'll find something. And if I don't, I'll think of something else," Brannon said, enthusiasm and motivation filling up inside her.

Silvia gave an approving nod.

"What can I do?" Blain asked.

"Help me," Brannon said, smiling.

"I have work this evening and for the next few days," I said. "Brannon could use your help, Blain."

"Sorted," Silvia said, "We have a week to figure this out before we head back to Heston."

"We can extend your stay," I said.

Silvia winked at us. She had a way of filling everyone with confidence. "That's kind, but I'm hoping we won't need to."

Brannon

Once Asher had gone to work, Blain and I started looking through the letters back in my cabin. I could tell he was excited and felt privileged to be helping me with this. I felt as though it was a good way to introduce him to supernatural life. I was also glad I didn't have to do it alone.

"What are we looking for?" he asked.

"Anything. Any knowledge about the Myst, the witches, any clue that could help to change the Myst. Anything I can take back to Juno as persuasion. Just, anything, really," I said.

We found nothing that night. We found nothing the next day and the next. All of the time spent reading fragile letters. There were so many more than I had realised on first looking at the box. Some had been folded up into squares, some had been ripped in half, which meant they didn't make sense until we found the other half. Some of them made sense, some of them made no sense at all.

I borrowed books from Asher's house and brought some of my own to the table, trying to decipher the letters as some were written in old English that I had no idea about. They were proving difficult, but they somehow linked together, and after much studying, I was finally able to make a breakthrough.

Dear Ancestor Selene Crescent,

It took hours of research to reveal that the Superiors were the vampire families. The Warlons, the Mastyeirs, the Crowlands and the Dregz. There were only four families, but they bred often, creating a huge community of vampires.

Selene

Blain asked his nan about this one. She was able to tell us that Simeon was a close friend of Juno's, despite being a Lunar witch. He knew that no one would overpower Juno and did not want to see his leader, who was also his good friend, lose her life for nothing.

To my fair lady,

I beg you, Selene. Do not join in the sacrifice. I cannot imagine a life without you. So empty, so sad. Your bravery is admirable but I do not love it now. Your silence is concerning for the Lunar witches. They will not sacrifice themselves, why should you? Come back to me, Selene. The battle has been won, and it has not been won by us.

You have my heart, forever.

Ancestor William

I was overcome by sadness when I read this one. Not only because Selene was loved so dearly, but because she gave up everything in her life, left behind a community of people who adored her, simply to ensure that the Lunar witches lived on. William might not realise how Selene's bravery did something. Neither of them knew that I planned to make it worth it.

"Brannon," Blain said handing me a thin sheet, "read this one."

Dear Ancestor Crescent,

I have heard the rumours of your decision to join us in the sacrifice. I feel compelled to inform you that the death of one Lunar witch will fail to have an impact. Whilst we have lived in peace, I have thoroughly enjoyed you as a friend. However, our

I had no words. On one hand, Juno did the right thing. She told Selene that her sacrifice wouldn't have an impact. In a way, she tried to preserve her life. However, Juno had an incredibly demanding manner and showed no hope at all in saving the Lunar witches.

The ink written words that spiralled and swirled down the rough pages forced me to reminisce about the time capsule I had to find for Juno. I enjoyed reading the letters then and I enjoyed reading these ones now. I felt like I was living through the 1600's with the witches, in a time when supernatural life was spoken about so ordinarily.

But as much as I enjoyed the letters, they were proving useless. Most of them were simply letters begging Selene to live. In the late afternoon of the third day, we had completed a read through of every letter, and to be honest, I was at a loss.

"Cup of tea?" Blain asked.

I nodded and lifted the box, about to start placing the hundreds of pieces of paper back in, when I realised there was a tightly folded piece of paper wedged into the seam of the lid.

The time has come. The sacrifice is tonight, and I shall be attending. I feel it necessary to write to you, as I have not left you without a way forward. I have indeed left hope. But it shall take some great perseverance to pursue.

The pendants that Juno created are two halves of the sun. The magic for the Myst will be stored in them, ensuring the survival of Sol witches and to the disadvantage of the Lunars.

After discussing with a powerful Curator witch, she decided to help me create a pendant of my own. The Crescent necklace.

I felt my heart surge and noticed my hands were shaking. Taking a breath, I read on.

When the sacrifice is made, and the spell of the Myst is chanted, I shall join in, clutching the Crescent necklace in my hand as I do so. My death, though nothing compared to the Sol clan, will mark the Earth with my power.

The Curator witch has helped me so that I will be able to redirect the power from my death into the necklace, but it will fall from my hands and be left in the spot of the sacrifice. My body will disappear into the afterlife.

It is crucial that the Crescent necklace is found by a Lunar witch and passed to my son, who I will miss dearly, and then to the children that come after him. The power of the necklace can only be released and controlled by my blood line. That was not my choice, I had hoped to have it for all Lunar witches, but sometimes the magic takes its own path.

The Queen of the Heavens is aware of my necklace, for the Curator witch did not want to betray her, but I am not sure what she will be able to do, for she too will disappear with me into the afterlife. If Ancestor Juno is not fond of the idea, she cannot change it. The deed is done.

It is with deep sadness that I feel the Myst will not welcome the Lunar witches with open arms. I am yet to discover what awaits me, but I am confident that we will unite once more, with the power that we sorely miss.

If, for whatever reason, an abundance of lunar power is needed, let the necklace guide you. It offers magic that Ancestor Juno does not have complete access to.

It has been my greatest honour to serve as your leading Ancestor, and my heart is heavy with the thought of being without you. However, I am sure that my sacrifice will, one day, be appreciated.

For now, it is farewell. I await your presence in death. Find my necklace.

My love, as always,

Ancestor Selene Crescent.

I was stunned. I looked across to where Blain was standing, making a cup of tea. The door opened and I jumped a little. Asher walked through the door, a broad smile on his face. I felt so energised that I nearly knocked him over as I ran to hug him.

"Wow, that's a nice welcome," he said, kissing me.

"It is, it is," I said and almost pushed him into a chair. "Listen, listen both of you." I stood in the middle of the room and read out Ancestor Selene's words from across the centuries. When I finished they were both staring at me.

"The crescent necklace," Asher said, "The one Blain has?"

Blain was leaning against the kitchen counter, his hand to his neck. "I'm not used to my jewellery being important," Blain said.

"And I'm not used to you being a Lunar witch descendant," I said.

Asher walked over to stand next to Blain, looking down at the pendant hanging around my best friend's neck. "So, Selene made this necklace and her death filled it with power. Clearly, someone did find it, and this letter, and gave them both to the Crescent family, which is why Silvia is in possession of them."

"It's one of her final sentences that I'm having trouble with. About Juno not having access to this power," Blain said.

"Well, I'd guess it's because Selene's power is lunar and Juno's is solar," Asher said.

"I think there's more to it than that," I said. "Do you remember Silvia telling us that Juno's mother was a Lunar witch? Juno must have some connection to Lunar power. But perhaps she needs the necklace to have it. Maybe Juno can't change the magic behind the Myst without a Lunar connection."

Our excitement grew as things started to make sense.

"Okay," Blain said, "what about the bit where she said to let it guide you?"

"I think she is saying follow your thoughts. Trust your instincts. Because the necklace will direct you in the right way," Asher said.

I looked at them both, suddenly knowing what to do. "I'm going to see Juno again," I announced. "But Blain, I need your necklace."

He took it off straight away and handed it to me. His complete and utter trust in me filled my heart with happiness and my head with confidence.

"What do you think she will say?" Asher asked.

"I'm not sure. But she can't give us the excuse that she can't fix it, because I think she can. With this," I said.

"It would make sense," Blain said. "Maybe she was so against the idea because she genuinely didn't know how to perform a spell affecting the Lunar witches without a lunar connection."

Asher

Brannon's eyes widened. "That's it!"

"What is?" I asked.

"The lunar connection," Brannon said. "Juno needs it to communicate with Selene. She needs her permission!"

The thrill in her voice at figuring this mess out was a sound that filled me with excitement. For her. For us. For the Lunar witches.

"Let's not get overly excited," Blain said. "Just in case nothing changes."

"Good point," I said.

"The letters told us multiple things. One of the most important is that Selene was very well respected. She was admired, loved even. She stood by the Lunar witches till the end," Brannon said. "She was a threat to Juno. She still is."

It was true. I had been taught that Juno was all these things. Respectable. Admirable. Loyal. Which she is. But Brannon's, and my, idea of loyal was not to the Sol witches. It was to all witches. And all the supernatural.

"We also learnt," Brannon continued, "That Selene's sacrifice wasn't a waste. Potentially, the power that was left by her death could be used to bring fairness to the Lunar witches, more than they even had before the Myst."

Blain smiled. "I need to tell my nan what we've figured out. I mean, it did take three days, lots of reading, and a sore back from sitting down for this long, but it was worth it. We have another chance."

He hugged us both lightly before returning to Silvia to let her know that faith was restored. There was the possibility of failure, but there always is.

Brannon packed up the letters into the box and placed the necklace in her shorts pocket.

"Can we go for a walk before we go?" I asked her. "I haven't seen you in days."

She smiled. "Of course."

I know she was eager to get things done, but this wasn't a forced smile. If she had missed me over these past days and wanted to spend some time with me rather than diving deep into our supernatural lives, then I was privileged.

We headed out. She was in her denim jean shorts and a lacy, white top. She looked prettier than yesterday. I think that every day.

The sun was beaming, just dipping on its journey to the horizon. It's vibrant yellow was soon becoming orange. The sky wasn't completely clear today. A few clouds were hovering over the sea, and the wind had picked up a little bit. Even still, there was no place I'd rather be.

We walked in silence for a while, simply enjoying each other's company. For the first time in a couple of weeks, we had things semi figured out. Brannon's shoulders had dropped, and the release of stress was visible.

We didn't verbalise where we were going. It's not like we had to. It would be the same place as always. Our favourite place.

Brannon

The waves collided harder than normal with the beams holding up the pier. As the navy-blue water crashed into the wood, the wave broke into spits of white froth and clear water. The intensity of the collision thrashed droplets of water onto our dangling legs.

It wasn't a peaceful evening, to be honest. The unsettled ocean was caused by a breeze that was stronger than normal. The sky, although patched with stunning colours, was cloudy, and the wind pushed those clouds on like they were late for some over the horizon appointment. There were people in the sea, but it wasn't as safe as normal to be playing in it. There was chatter coming from the beach, but no sign of youthful laughter or innocent freedom.

"Maybe a storm is brewing," Asher said.

"Maybe," I said.

He looked at me, as if everything around us had disappeared and the only concern he had was my eyes. How deeply he could look into them. It was as if he was trying to look through them, past the pools of purple and lilac and into my chaotic mind. I wasn't in a reserved or quiet mood, so he wouldn't have to dig for answers tonight.

"Do you think Juno will agree to help?" he asked, his voice raspy and soft.

"Honestly, I have no idea. Part of me thinks no, because, with the necklace or not, she is risking the community of the Myst's respect for her. Some people will not like the Lunar witches to be equal to them. They'll blame Juno if she changes anything, and the peace that she's created will be disturbed. But part of me also thinks yes, because how can she justifiably not," I said.

"I agree," Asher said.

"How are you feeling about it?" I asked, realising that I didn't ask him enough.

He pondered for a moment. "Nervous," he admitted. "If she says no, then I'm afraid we might have to give up and let things be. And that makes me nervous because I know you won't be able to stop."

"Do you hate that about me?" I asked, my insecurity displaying itself.

"Not at all," he said. "I mean, sure, you can be demanding. You're persistent and pretty much relentless. You care so deeply about it that it has more control over your emotions than I'd like it to have. But I don't hate it. If anyone needed something doing, I'd send them your way. Because this side of you is also confident and trustworthy. Reliable. Consistent. So many things that I value."

"I don't know how you put up with me," I said, with a breathy laugh.

"I don't know how I'm lucky enough to get to put up with you," he said.

He placed his hand on my thigh and spread his fingers. My heart leaped. His touch was electric.

I stared at him as he admired the setting sun. His sharp jawline appeared so firm and contrasted with his delicate and caring ocean blue eyes. He was a view that I'd never be able to get enough of. Timeless.

"I feel very lucky, too," I told him. "To have you."

I wanted to say more. I wanted to tell him that he completed me, in every possible way. That his presence in my life made me the luckiest girl alive. That I didn't care where we were, or how much money we had, I'd love him. I'd love him to the death. But I didn't say anything.

Asher

She looked at me, her eyes bursting with love. And although she didn't say anything, I knew.

"Shall we go now?" I asked.

She nodded. We headed to our quiet spot on the beach and caught one last glimpse of the sun. It had melted into the horizon, a golden half still above the ocean. A familiar sight that I'd see in the seconds after I opened my eyes.

And there it was. The crimson sky, half of the sun and the still waters of the Myst.

Juno strode across to us. It seemed this was no time for her to gently saunter. I immediately used my powers and pushed my mind into the future. There was no explosive argument or storming off to come, but I couldn't see much else. Maybe we would be fine, and she was just anxious about what we would say. What Brannon would say.

"Hi Juno," Brannon said, in a sweet and slightly forced voice that I did know wouldn't last long.

Juno smiled, but it lacked any sincerity.

"Miss Amory. Mr Curator. Back so soon?"

"Hello, Juno," I said. "I think Brannon has found a way to make afterlife fair for all witches. We just need you to get on board."

Her smile, false or not, evaporated.

"In the kindest way possible, I told you I couldn't help. My words were true. And there is nothing to fix," Juno said.

Brannon's posture straightened. She stared directly into Juno's eyes and her voice lost all sweetness. "There is plenty to fix, Juno, and, *in the kindest way possible*, I should tell you that I won't stop. Not until you've tried," Brannon said and her sarcastic use of Juno's own words weren't lost on me, or Juno.

My heart pounded with pride. She was so caring but would stand her ground against anyone for the greater good. We knew the history and the facts, and we had knowledge that we'd never had before. Juno would have to put up more than a fight to change our minds about this, especially Brannon and her head strong attitude.

"Miss Amory, do you understand how much I'm putting at risk?" Juno asked.

"Yes. You're risking how much people like you. How much they respect you. The peace that you've created in the afterlife. I get it," Brannon said. "But I don't think you understand how much happiness you could bring to so many witches. How many more people would like you and respect you."

Juno struggled for words. "What about the peace, Miss Amory? It will be gone."

"You don't know that, but if that's what happens, then let it go," Brannon said, simply. "You'll have to let it go."

"I'm sorry, but I cannot do that," Juno said. "Besides, it is physically impossible for me to change the magic to that extent."

"It was," I said.

"Before you had this," Brannon added, dangling the Crescent necklace in her hand.

"Where did you get that?" Juno said, mesmerised by the necklace and in shock that Brannon was holding it.

"Blain," Brannon said. "My best friend. The one whose nan, Silvia Crescent, informed us about the Lunar witches."

Silence fell, and a curious thought came to me. We three, here at this moment, how much power had we accumulated? Juno, the Queen of the Heavens. The pendant holders, who now have magical abilities. The pendants. The necklace. Surely, we could do anything.

"You understand that this belonged to Ancestor Selene Crescent?" Juno asked. "I cannot do anything with this."

Her lack of eye contact and the break in her voice would have told us she was lying, even if we hadn't had the knowledge that we did.

"Juno, please," I said, "don't treat us like idiots."

She looked taken aback. It was usually Brannon who was unfiltered and straight to the point. But I'd had enough. I nodded for Brannon to tell her.

"Juno, I've spent days reading letters from Lunar witches to Selene. She kept them in a box, and they were handed down the family. It was a bit like your time capsule. After hearing how well respected and widely admired Selene was, I knew she would have done more than sacrificed herself," Brannon said.

"I, eventually, found a letter that she had written to the Lunar witches before her death, explaining this necklace. It took some guess work, but I think that you need to use this necklace to communicate with her, and to find a way to change things."

"Very good, Miss Amory. You are extremely intelligent for someone who only recently learnt about the supernatural world. I do need the necklace to communicate with Ancestor Selene. I also need it to engage with Lunar power. Two things required of me if I was to alter the Myst," Juno said.

Brannon's eyes lightened. She had hope, and a lot of it.

"Is Ancestor Selene in the Myst?" I asked.

"Yes," Juno said. "But I am yet to come face to face with her. I can admit that I have not exactly been looking for her, though."

"Do you have any idea where she is?" Brannon asked.

"I'm afraid not. She has been in hiding for four centuries. I believe she acted this way to ensure that I could only communicate with her through the necklace, or through spells that she had to grant me permission to use," Juno said. "Miss Amory I must ask what you intend to achieve from this. What is it that you want me to change?"

"Isn't it obvious?" Brannon asked. "I want the Lunar witches to be able to perform magic all the time, at their full strength, like Sol witches."

"Why?" Juno asked bluntly, obviously not thinking this was a great idea.

"Because it's not fair. Imagine yourself in their shoes. You wait your entire life, living like an ordinary human but knowing that you're far more. When death greets you, instead of confidently knowing that you can now embrace a life as a witch, you are filled with uncertainty. And then disappointed by the truth. You can't be like the other witches. You can't do magic. You have to continue to live a human-like life in a supernatural afterlife, watching people with the same abilities as you use those abilities, whilst you aimlessly and lifelessly survive."

Brannon's words struck a chord with Juno. Her hard glare softened, and something that Brannon said had broken through her refusal. It was like she could see, finally, what we could see.

Brannon continued. "Juno, I understand this is a risk. But if you don't try to change this, I will be removing my pendant."

I was the one in shock now.

"If you remove the pendant, you can't be with Mr Curator," Juno said.

"I know," Brannon said. She looked at me and took my hand. "Asher, I love you more than I've ever loved before. You complete me. You make me the luckiest girl alive, and I don't care where we are or what we have, I'll love you to death. But I can't be that selfish that I'd put my desire above what's right. And you know what's right is for the Lunar witches to have the same afterlife as every other supernatural being."

My heart sunk but her reasoning kept it afloat. Whilst it pained me to think of a life without her, I did understand that the Lunar witches had to come first, I guess.

I nodded. She kissed my cheek. I melted at the touch of her lips. No amount of time with her would ever be enough.

"I don't appreciate your threats, Miss Amory, but fine," Juno said, "I will try."

I thought I'd heard her wrong, but I hadn't. She said that. She said she'd try.

"I would not forgive myself if my stubborn and selfish worries ended the love between the pendant holders. Even if it hadn't been four hundred years in the waiting, I would not see the two of you part. Not at the fault of myself," Juno said.

The smile on Brannon's face was one I'd never seen before. It was bursting. To the point I thought it might escape her face.

Juno continued. "But, Miss Amory, if the peace in the Myst is disrupted. You will be the one to help me restore it."

Brannon smiled. As if that would phase her, now.

"Thank you, Juno," Brannon said. "And I apologise for how demanding I was."

"Well," Juno said, breaking into a smile as she held Brannon's gaze, "Shy kids get no sweets."

Brannon

I couldn't believe it. Juno agreed to try. That was good enough for me. Besides, she's Juno. Trying is equivalent to succeeding. She made the Myst, after all.

"What do we do now?" Asher asked.

"I'm going to keep the necklace and try to communicate with Ancestor Selene. Hopefully, we can unite together and compose a spell to alter the magic of the Myst. Now, I must make you both aware. I cannot predict the outcome of this. I cannot tell you how the Myst may look after the deed is done. It is essential that you know this, because I cannot make promises about something so unpredictable," Juno stated.

We both nodded in understanding.

"Furthermore, if and when we have a spell prepared, I will be proposing the idea to the community of supernatural beings in the Myst before proceeding with the changes. It is important that the majority agree this is right. It has always been my greatest effort to ensure that the Myst is run as a democracy, not a dictatorship," she said.

We nodded again, although I was concerned that this would be harder to achieve.

"I will call for you both when I am ready. Be prepared."

"Thanks, Juno," I said.

"Bye," Asher said, as Juno prepared to walk back through the sun, the phrase we used instead of walking into death.

"Miss Amory, Mr Curator, I will see you both soon."

With that, she raised her hood over her wispy silver hair and walked away. We watched, in silence, until she was out of sight.

"Well," Asher said, "you did it!"

He picked me up in his embrace and swung me around in celebration.

"No," I said, "we did it."

I pressed my lips on his. Then, we shut our eyes and returned to reality.

We came back around, smiles still plastered on our faces. Asher was looking up at the sky. It was dark now. The moon was less full than a couple of nights ago, surrounded by a million dotted stars. The brightest star, I imagined, would be a blinding white up close. I stared at it for a while.

"He'd be proud of you, you know," Asher said.

I looked into his eyes and found comfort in his words. It would hurt. Forever. But on nights like this, after experiencing supernatural milestones like this, I knew Asher was right. He would be proud.

Asher

The following morning, we informed Silvia and Blain about our interaction with Juno and the success that we'd had. They were, appropriately, over the moon, especially Silvia. She cried and gave us long, heartfelt hugs.

What neither Brannon nor I had anticipated was how the wait would feel, wondering when Juno would summon us.

The first day was spent with Silvia and Blain. We went to the beach to watch a paddle boarding competition and had cheeseburgers and chips, accompanied by lots of fruity cocktails. The atmosphere was great. Everyone was excited and glad to have some entertainment. We finished the day off with dinner at my house. My mum laid out an Italian style grazing board, with all sorts of ham, cheeses, olives and crackers. My dad and Silvia discussed all things supernatural, and how devastating it was that he had no idea about the Lunar witches. Then we sat around our fire pit, Silvia providing us with comical stories of Brannon and Blain's childhood, like when they got hold of face paints and covered each other in blue and orange swirls. Brannon managed to paint Blain's entire arm green, and Blain refused to take it off, crying and having a tantrum on the floor when Silvia approached him with a wipe. Or on their first day of primary school, when they told their teachers they were twins. The truth was revealed when Silvia was called to the school to pick up her poorly granddaughter because they couldn't get in contact with her parents. At first, she thought they'd got confused. However, she quickly had to clear up the fact that she was not a guardian of Brannon's, let alone her nan.

On the second day I had to work with my dad. We had one coach load of people leaving before two more coaches arrived. I had to monitor reception for both the checkouts and check-ins as well as move a few rooms around to accommodate families. Then I had to help some elderly ladies on a 'girls holiday', up to their rooms with their excessive luggage. It seemed at times that the camp duties were never-ending, as once all that was done, I had to arrange a month's worth of evening entertainment, contacting every band, comedian, magician and dance group that I could find. This took the longest time, and I was convinced that I double booked multiple days, so had to revise my work about ten times. Once night had fallen, I helped the cleaners mop the floor of reception and water the indoor plants. It was a long, distracting day.

Not for Brannon, though. She had to occupy herself and so took Silvia and Blain into town, showing them the souvenir shops. Silvia purchased five magnets, eight pens and two mugs, all with 'Greece' spelled out in big blue letters. In the evening, Brannon and Blain went to the cocktail hut for some *blue lagoons*. They popped in on their walk home and helped me to water the indoor plants. Then they went to Brannon's cabin, where Blain stayed the night, and they did a facemask. Sometimes I was glad Blain could distract her like that. I loved her, but facemasks weren't really my scene.

Brannon helped me with camp duties the next day, whilst Blain and his nan went for another day at the beach. We spent the morning walking down the beach, picking up litter. After her familiar rant about how selfish and inconsiderate people were to leave their empty bottles and food packages on the beach, we spoke about more positive things. We discussed her garden and how good it looked now, some plans I had for improving camp and, inevitably, if we thought Juno had been successful so far. The afternoon was spent helping the cleaners make beds and refresh the bathrooms. We were pretty much into summer now and this time of year demanded major adjustments to cleaning schedules as there was so much more to do. Brannon wanted to help, so I introduced her to how we worked out the system. Once that was done, we got an early night, falling asleep to a film.

I remember my last thought was, 'Hurry up Juno. Please hurry up.'

Brannon

The final day of waiting felt like the longest. I started the morning off with a walk up the mountain, mentally noting that the walking path could do with some weeding and gardening skills applied to it. Then I discussed extending Silvia and Blain's stay with reception, ensuring that they didn't book that cabin for at least two more weeks. I had no idea how long Juno would take, or if changing the Myst would be a process. I know it would be easy to phone Blain to let him know, but I felt like he and his nan deserved to be present and close whilst it happened.

I spent the rest of the day in my garden with Blain and Silvia, sunbathing and occasionally having a dip in the pool, or floating around aimlessly on an inflatable crocodile. It dragged. I was desperate, to know what was happening. It was almost a week and we had heard nothing. I would be lying if I said I didn't have any concerns. Juno might've changed her mind and been too scared to tell us. She might've never meant it in the first place.

Asher joined us mid-afternoon, after his morning shift at work. He had changed into chino shorts and a black t-shirt. He looked handsome, as always, and I was glad that just before I'd started making lunch, I'd thrown on a strappy black dress. I liked to look good for him.

We enjoyed our food and were preparing to resume our sunbathing. Silvia was turning a dark brown with only tanning oil applied. I felt envious, and Blain was annoyed that he was turning a scarlet red shade.

We were sitting on my sun beds when Asher's eyes flickered to a close. Maybe I should have felt worried, or nervous, but I didn't. I felt excited. It was only a moment until my mind was pulled to another place and my vision blurred to total blackness. I was relieved that Silvia and Blain knew what was happening and would be waiting in anticipation for our return.

My eyes were warmly greeted by the same sight I'd seen all my life. I think part of me expected something different, as if things would've changed by now. But it was the same. A crimson sky streaked with tangerine sun beams over a still turquoise ocean. Next to me was Asher, his chestnut curls looser than normal but nesting on his head perfectly. In front of me was Juno. Her eyes glistening and her fidgety smile, desperately trying to conceal what I could see was good news.

"Ancestor Selene agreed," she said, the words bursting out of her.

I felt my jaw tingling with excitement. The Myst was going to change forever.

"You have a spell?" Asher asked, mirroring my excitement.

Juno took our hands in hers and squeezed them.

"We think so," she said, "We have created a spell that allows us to alter the Myst. It will, if it works, allow us to welcome lunar power into the Myst, allowing Lunar witches to perform magic at all times, like the Sol witches. It will take great power to do this, so I, therefore, have something to ask you both."

"You're not going to ask us to sacrifice ourselves, are you?" Asher asked. He said it in a humorous way, but I was glad our minds thought alike.

Juno laughed softly. "No, Mr Curator. The spell is a demanding one, but I can confirm that no sacrifice is necessary. We are attempting to alter the rules of the supernatural afterlife rather than create it. It does not require as much power, though it does still need a lot.

"My ask of you both, Miss Amory and Mr Curator, is that you participate in the spell, if it is to go ahead."

I could sense that Asher felt apprehensive about this. I understood why. We had grown up knowing that we were a force of supernatural power, but we never would have guessed that the leading Ancestor of all witches would one day ask us to participate in her spell. Partly, it was terrifying. But, for me, it was where I wanted to be, now. In the centre of it all.

"We don't know spells or magic," Asher said, his expression revealing his confusion.

"Mr Curator, I will not require either of you to know magic, nor the spell. The power in your pendants, now in yourselves, too, is what I'd like to have access to. Your bodies and the pendants share four hundred years' worth of built-up power. It would allow us plenty enough to perform the spell," Juno said.

"How do we do that?" I asked. "How do we give our power to you?"

"Selene and I will take one of your hands. Your other hand will hold the pendant. We will siphon the magic from the pendant, through and of your body, into ourselves, whilst chanting the spell. Then, we can await the change and hope, patiently, that our spell is successful," Juno said.

"So, what did Ancestor Selene say?" I asked, curious to know.

"Ancestor Selene Crescent was overjoyed. She was highly surprised that a Sol witch was fighting for the rights of the Lunar witches. She was also surprised that I had listened to you,

Miss Amory. I assured her," Juno said, "that it was not a decision I made lightly, or without hesitation."

I smiled as she raised her eyebrows at me. I knew I had challenged her to do something that she didn't imagine she'd ever have to face. But I knew that she respected me for doing it. She viewed me as a younger version of herself and I, sometimes, felt as though I was pushing for things that she wished she had. Juno was good at composing herself. Her demeanour was calm and settled. But it was obvious. She was, in this moment, excited. As excited as me and Asher. It made me wonder whether these were regrets of Juno's that she was glad to be correcting. Or, at least, trying to make right.

"Mr Curator, Miss Amory, can I confirm that your participation can be relied upon?" Juno asked.

Asher turned to me. "Are you okay with that?" he asked.

"I am. Are you?" I asked.

He nodded. "You can count on us, Juno."

"I thought so," Juno said. "Now, as told before, it is important to me that the people of the Myst are on board with this. So, we will be heading there shortly, for the first gathering of the Ancestors in four centuries!" Juno clapped her hands in excitement.

Words escaped me. I felt as though I'd misunderstood. In fact, I was sure I had. "What do you mean?" I asked her. "We can't go past the borderline."

"With me, you can. Which is also made far easier by the cooperation of Ancestor Selene," Juno said.

"We're going into the Myst?" Asher asked, his mind exploding with questions and shock.

"Yes, Mr Curator. How else do you suppose you will talk with the Ancestors?"

Asher

If I was to guess how this conversation would've gone, it would not have been like this. I couldn't quite comprehend it. I couldn't believe it. The afterlife that I had anchored my entire life, only seeing the borderline of, was now open to me to see. It didn't feel possible.

I knew that it was possible. Juno created the Myst. She could, pretty much, manipulate the rules whenever she wanted. But part of me was worried. Walking into the Myst was the final thing one did before officially passing into death. What if we didn't come back?

"How do you know we will get out again?" Brannon asked.

It was as if she'd read my mind. She must've guessed from reading into my emotions that this was my concern.

"I will accompany you out again. Ancestor Selene Crescent is on standby, if anything was to prevent your exit, as a precautionary measure," Juno said.

There wasn't much left to be said. Juno was beginning to walk towards the water, and we had to follow. I was nervous about what would be on the other side. The next hurdle that we would have to fight our way over.

My feet touched the water and I realised how strange an experience this was going to be. I was pushing my legs through the sea, but they didn't get wet. Whilst I could feel the wetness, my shoes remained dry. I noticed how Brannon was struggling with this feeling too. It was one that I couldn't get my head around.

I wondered, for a moment, if this happened to everyone who passed through. I realised I'd never noticed anyone with soaking wet clothing or uncomfortable, clinging material. I can imagine that they were too distracted by dying to be too bothered about this sensation, but it disturbed me.

The sun got larger as we got closer. I struggled to look at it, the brightness causing my eyes to sting. I reached for Brannon's hand. She turned to me, a smile still on her face. I got the impression that she wasn't overly bothered by any of this. Not in a negative way. She was thrilled at the opportunity. She was embracing it. The gleam in her eyes made me want to embrace it too. To enjoy it how she did.

Brannon

If this was how it felt to die, then it scared me far less than it had done before. I understand that there would be so much to leave behind, but there's more to look forward to. For the supernatural.

I wished that everyone could experience this. A distorted reality. A place where everything you believed to be true is not.

As a child, it played on my mind a lot. What happened after death. It's a topic we all wonder about. We all crave an answer. I used to tell myself that I'd see my family in a place above the sky, and we'd laugh all day, watching over the people we left behind, waiting for them to grow their wings and join us. I suppose the Myst is like that in many ways. Seeing your family.

I put an end to this thought immediately. Juno made it clear that she had never seen my dad. His body was homing excess power. He couldn't return. He didn't get his second chance.

The sun was blinding. It felt like we were so close, yet the walk felt like a long one.

My thoughts spiralled in every direction. Why is everyone scared of fire but not of the sun? They're both extremely hot. And dangerous. They share the same colour palette, a blood orange concoction with burnt marigold sparks. It was a pointless thought, I decided. There were more important things to ponder on.

Like, is this how it feels to die? Are you too overwhelmed by the experience to feel the sadness? Or are you too lost in sadness to appreciate the experience? After living a normal, human life, is it a long-awaited feeling to be treated as more in death?

The silence was deafening. Juno had done this many times before, but this was foreign to me and Asher. Everything was quiet but my mind. My mind was the opposite.

It got to the point where I had to look down at my legs, which were now nearly completely absorbed in the ocean, because the sun was too bright. The water was level with my thighs, although I only knew that because I looked. I couldn't feel it. Whilst the motion of walking through water felt the same, my legs and my dress were dry.

It's magic, I guess. The Myst isn't a place on Earth. It's a place built by witches. A spell. Maybe what Asher and I had always admired, the view, was not really there at all. It was a disguised passageway, invented to calm you down and sooth your suffering. A glorified death.

Even though I was staring into the sea, the blinding light from the sun surrounded my vision. I squinted, barely able to keep my eyes open a fraction, , feeling them start to water. It was unbearable.

Then, suddenly, it stopped. The blinding light disappeared. I no longer had to force one leg in front of the other. The feeling had gone. I opened my eyes.

We were here. In the Myst.

Asher

We were standing on a beach. I turned around. The sun was still half set, but now behind us. The ocean was as still as it normally is. The sky was scarlet and crimson. It was a direct reflection of where we had just come from.

This was surreal.

I looked ahead. There was a cliff. It wasn't too big, and I noticed a flight of stairs leading to the top. Then I noticed the village.

We climbed the stairs, following Juno.

Each step was full of wonder about what awaited us at the top. As the final step was taken, I saw up close what I had seen from a distance.

The village was small, but I knew this wouldn't be the whole of the Myst. There were far too many supernatural deaths for everyone to live here.

There was a block of buildings. It felt like I was in a movie as I read the names. 'Welcome Witches', 'Vampire Entry', 'Werewolf Settling' and 'Other Arrivals'.

"It is probably clear that when you arrive in the Myst, you must enter the appropriate building for your introduction to the afterlife. It's where you learn the laws and gain an understanding of life here," Juno said. "Or death." She chuckled.

We followed her to the left and walked along the cliff's edge. The distant horizon was lined with what appeared to be another village.

There were beautiful cottages amongst ordinary bungalows and houses. There were vast stretches of green land, dotted with colourful flowers and ancient-looking trees. There was a stream running down the centre, with Lilli pads and fishing rods. The stream led to a lake, with several mini piers creating walkways to fishing bays, or very small boats like the ones at the lagoon. It was peaceful and quiet and pleasant.

"There are many, many villages," Juno said. "This is a rather serene one. The intention of it is to make the adjustment from human life to supernatural life easier. A place to settle in."

We continued walking. Everything went by so fast. I had barely enough time to take it all in.

Juno led us to the next village along. Although, it wasn't really a village. It was her home.

Her house was colossal. Great pillars framed the house and gold lined every harsh edge or corner. It was so clean and, other than the gold, dazzling white. The doorway was at the back of a courtyard. Rooms ran along the edges of the courtyard, and I peeked in the windows. There were rich, purple carpets and grand dining tables. It looked like royalty lived here. And of course, it did.

"A lot of magic is practiced in my premises," she said. "I have many facilities, and I grow many necessary herbs for spells. I enjoy when the witches gather to practice magic, and I enjoy, even more, to teach them what I know."

Brannon's face had lit up since we got here. She looked at the Myst in the same way she looks at me. Completely in love.

"How big is the Myst?" Brannon asked.

"That's a difficult question to answer. I would estimate that at the moment, it's the size of the United Kingdom," Juno said. "There is lots to see. Many environments which the different supernatural breeds like to inhabit, but we are not here for a tour, I need to change into appropriate attire before the gathering begins."

"But, Juno, so many people die. How does the Myst accommodate everyone?" Brannon asked.

"The Myst can respond to new arrivals. It changes. It grows as it needs to, it is as small as a village or as huge as a continent, however many deaths there are. But it is important to note that this afterlife is a choice," Juno said, answering my next question. "No one is forced to stay here. One may choose to leave straight away, or after a decade, or never. This is not every being's idea of peace. But it is an opportunity to explore one's magical abilities for as long as they desire." She smiled. "I shan't be long."

Brannon and I shared a look. We were clearly both overwhelmed and couldn't find adequate words.

"How are you feeling?" Brannon asked me.

"This is crazy. I can't believe we were sat in your garden half an hour ago and now we are in the Myst," I said. "How are you feeling?"

"Nervous," she said.

"Why?"

"Because I had no time to prepare. I don't know what to say to all these Ancestors. I need to convince them that this is the right thing to do. It's so obvious to me, but I don't know how I'm going to makes them realise it."

This was when I realised that our feelings of being overwhelmed were not shared. I was overwhelmed because this was too new. This was scary, to me. And part of me was

desperate to go home. Reality is comfortable and I wanted it
back.

Brannon

I knew he felt that way, but I couldn't relate. I was overwhelmed in a good way. This was an experience that I wouldn't have again. My first time in the Myst. Walking around a supernatural village. Standing outside of Juno's house and witching courtyard. I was exhilarated. I was immersed in it. It was escapism from normality. To think that I could reassure any future beings who passed through that I've been there and it's lovely. It didn't faze me like it did Asher. I wasn't feeling lost or confused.

Reality *is* comfortable. And I didn't want it back. I needed to find some confidence. I needed to represent myself positively to the Ancestors.

"Don't be nervous," Asher said. "It only took me one look at you for my heart to decide you're the one. You're the most persuasive person I know."

He took me around the waist and pulled me closer. This was something I adored about him. Even though we weren't on the same page, he continued to love me as if I were the words to his favourite story. We weren't on the same page, but he loved the book all the same.

"I don't want to persuade them with my face, or make them fall for me," I said, placing my hands on the top of his arms. "I want to prove that—"

"That you're not that bad Amory Ancestor who they all despise."

I nodded.

"Listen to me," he said. "Some of these Ancestors are going to hate the idea of equality for all witches. They're going to tear the idea down, and they're going to bring you down with it. But promise me one thing."

"What?"

"That you will not be ashamed of your surname."

I smiled. He was everything. And more than that.

"If they knew Juno was an Amory, their opinions would change rapidly," he continued. "So, promise me you'll own it."

I sighed, and a giggle slipped out. He filled me with happiness. He gave me confidence.

"I promise."

He began to kiss me, but it was only seconds until we heard Juno's door close. We immediately let go of each other and backed away, as if one of our parents had walked into our bedrooms at an inconvenient time.

The moment I saw her was the moment it truly sunk in. We were in another world.

She wore a full length cloak, made from a violet silk material that looked polished in the sunlight. Her hair was slicked back into a bun at the base of her skull. Her head was tilted, her chin pointing up, so she carried herself in a proud, commanding way. She embodied my vision of a witch, without the pointy hat and broomstick.

She was an Amory. The maker of this place. Her blood ran through my veins.

We were family.

Asher

"Mr Curator, Miss Amory," Juno said, nodding at us both. "Will you kindly follow me to the gathering of the Ancestors?"

Standing before her, when she looked like this, felt different. Replacing the dull, black cloak was a good move. A powerful move. Her presence was intimidating. She truly was a leader.

We followed her back to the flight of stairs carved into the cliff. Her cloak trailed behind her, lifting off the floor with every proud step she took.

We walked along the beach. I held Brannon's hand, squeezing it every time she looked at me, her eyes full of nerves. I knew she'd be fine and I hoped my hand in hers reassured her.

"We are almost there," Juno said. "We should be set up in this bay."

The cliff curved into a small sized cove. As we walked around the corner, Brannon's nerves became contagious. My legs could have collapsed.

There were eyes. So many beady eyes, staring us up and down.

The Ancestors were already here. There were row upon row of chairs laid out on the sand, all of them occupied. I thought Juno was intimidating, but this was far worse.

We walked to the front, where a grand chair, like a throne, stood, flanked by two smaller versions of itself.

All the faces that stared at us were sombre. No one smiled. No one broke their gaze. The spotlight was on us. For the first time in four centuries, the pendant holders were here. In front of them once more.

The majority were old. Unlike Juno, these people all wore pointy black hats and black cloaks. I assumed this was the Ancestor's uniform. But under their hats I saw white and grey hair, thin and aged. A lot of them had wrinkles. Not weak, ugly wrinkles. No. They were more like signs of wisdom, engraved on their faces.

I took in their appearance but did not make eye contact. I felt as though my eyes would display my terror as weakness and, for some reason, I didn't want them to think I was weak. Brannon was feeling pressure because of her surname and now, so was I. I felt as though I had a lot to live up to. The Curator Ancestor was respected. My family had always been a great source of power. The Ancestors would still expect that because they had no idea what the Curator family stood for in the Modern World. I couldn't let them down.

I looked at Brannon. Clearly, my fear of making eye contact was not shared by her. She was looking everyone in the eye. Not with arrogance or with the intention of bragging. That wasn't her. Her eye contact was due to her genuine curiosity. I could read it on her face. How absorbed she was by it all.

Juno's walk stayed the same. She did not look at the Ancestors. She looked ahead, striding with confidence and power. She headed straight for her throne, a gold edged chair with gold legs and a white, velvet cushion. She turned to me and Brannon to indicate that we should sit either side of her.

I walked to the one farthest away and let Brannon have the closer one. She sat down, still taking in the faces of everyone in front. After helping Juno up the step to her throne, I sat and finally looked into the eyes of the Ancestors.

"Well, then," Juno said. "Let us begin."

Brannon

"Let me, firstly, introduce you to the people we owe a great, great debt to. Miss Amory and Mr Curator, the pendant holders who we must thank for reawakening the Myst. By choosing love, they chose us. For that, we shall be eternally grateful."

There was silence as a hundred eyes scanned me and Asher. My paranoia told me that it was mostly me, though. Juno raised her hands and began to clap them together. It was awkward and slow. The Ancestors began to join in, but it was not a round of applause. It was a sound of uncomfortable and forced clapping, peppered with a few enthusiastic efforts too.

"Miss Amory, Mr Curator, let me introduce you, now, to the Ancestors. We are joined today by my most loyal and faithful friends. The witches and sorcerers that I trust above all others. We are also joined by the four Superior leaders, who I am sure you know are the vampire families, and the alphas of the werewolves. My dear friends, it is so good to gather together once more."

The Ancestors bowed their heads, there was some cheering for Juno. For the first time, smiles appeared.

"We are also joined by members of the Myst who wanted to participate in the gathering."

I thought I would feel frightened. There were vampires and werewolves sitting in front of me, but I didn't care. I wasn't frightened. I was ready.

I briefly dipped into my powers, trying to gather how the Ancestors were feeling. A lot of them were in disbelief, which made sense. Asher and I were the pendant holders. We awoke the Myst and granted them an afterlife. A lot of them were grateful. Some were suspicious. Weary. Amazed. Inspired. Overjoyed. So many emotions that their faces failed to tell.

"I have brought the pendant holders into the Myst today because a suggestion has been made," Juno said. She inhaled and exhaled deeply, in preparation to begin the explanation. "As you are aware, the Lunar witches failed to join us in the sacrifice, aside from Ancestor Crescent. Selene Crescent." Chatter erupted amongst the crowd. Her name caused faces to change, eyebrows to scrunch, eyes to widen. Juno raised her voice above the noise. "Her interference, as history proves, did not affect this afterlife, but her presence is felt." A few heads turned to the sun. Half of the sun. "The Lunar witches do not get to do magic here like the rest of us. Unlike everyone gathered here today, they are unable to explore their supernatural abilities, something we all await when passing into the Myst. A question has been raised. Is this fair?"

The chatter erupted again, louder this time. Some people gestured their disagreement by throwing about their hands whilst others sat still and listened. I guessed that these people were eager to hear the suggestion and, possibly, eager to agree.

"I understand that some of you may believe that this is not something that needs to be changed. However, after imagining how I would feel if I was a Lunar witch, I came to the conclusion that, perhaps, the Myst could do with some altering.

"Once, I united us all. The witches survived in the same community. In fact, we did more than survive. We thrived, as neighbours. I see no harm in trying to achieve this again.

"The Myst is a safe place, free from conflict or war. The Lunar witches cannot harm the Sol witches, and vice versa. Therefore, I believe that this change would be a good one, allowing us the opportunity to expand the witching community and bring fairness to the supernatural afterlife.

"Now you may have your say. Please kindly raise your hand if you would like to speak, and your queries will be answered by one of the three of us. I will say that the two young, but very intelligent, people before you are pendant holders, and the only two beings in the Modern World to have powers in four hundred years. Their say is very significant, and they will be heard."

The Ancestors all removed their hats, clearly something they used to do in these gatherings when Juno had finished talking. Now I could see to the very back row, and started to recognise faces of those I had guided into the Myst.

Asher

I couldn't miss her warm smile. Her grey hair was clipped up in the same way, and her cheeks were as rosy as I remembered. It was Flo.

"I'll tell you one thing, Mr Curator. Behind every good man, is an even better woman. Find an amazing girl and let her make you a better man."

I could hear her raspy voice. I remembered her well. How cheeky she was, and her jokes about her husband. But then I noticed her hand. It was being held by an elderly gentleman.

A lump grew in my throat, and goose bumps appeared on my arms. He'd joined her.

She noticed me smiling at both of them. She winked at me. I didn't feel nervous anymore.

Brannon

The resemblance was uncanny. Long black hair, knotted down past the seat of the chair. Piercing dark eyes that made my heart beat a little faster. Two identical, unwelcoming smiles. It was the Westman twins, died in 1624. Killed in the witch trials, despite being found innocent.

I remembered meeting Mrs Westman to get Juno's necklace in Heston. How she hated me because I was an Amory. By the evil stare the twins were giving me, I could tell this hatred had been passed down the family.

Asher

Then there was Chris, the werewolf. I had to let him down when he passed through me. The pendants were too far apart when Brannon was in Heston and the Myst was paused. He had no idea how long he'd have to wait until he could experience life as a werewolf.

He arrived so optimistic and left so disappointed. But he's here now. And his smile told me that he didn't hate me for delaying this experience for him.

Brannon

A lot of the Ancestors wore necklaces with their surname on. I assumed this was something that used to be popular in the Old World.

I skimmed through them, recognising a few from the letters I had read in Juno's time capsule. Liza, Edwardo, Baylen. I felt like I knew them, even though we'd never met.

Hands began to rise in the air, some with confidence, others hesitantly.

"Ancestor Hitchin," Juno said, acknowledging a man in the front row.

He stood up and bowed to Juno.

"Queen of the Heavens, it is my honour to stand before you. My concern would be how the Lunar witches would assimilate into our already developed society. Would there be unrest or difficulty?" he asked.

I waited for Juno's answer but failed to notice that, all the while, she was looking to me, expecting me to be the one to talk. Asher noticed and stepped in.

"Erm, hi," Asher said, very awkwardly. "I don't think the Lunar witches would struggle to fit in. They are witches after all, and belong in a supernatural environment like this one."

The man sat down, seeming satisfied with Asher's answer.

Another hand shot up. Another man, but he was glaring at me in an unfriendly way.

"Ancestor Juno, I see no problem with the way things are now. It never occurred to anyone as a problem, until *she* brought it up. Would it be fair to suggest that this girl is looking for attention? Perhaps, to meddle in something that she has no place meddling in?"

It felt like a punch in the throat. A chatter sprung up through the rows of seats. Asher gripped his chair so hard that I didn't need to channel my powers to know he was fuming. But the pressure was on, and I had to respond. I thought about what Asher said. To own it.

I stood. "Hi, Sir," I began. "Thank you for raising your concern. I think the best way to approach this issue is to let everyone have their say and share their opinions. But would it be fair to say that your, quite disrespectful, opinion has been targeted at me because I'm an Amory?"

All the chatter stopped, and silence fell. I continued to make eye contact with the man. He struggled to hold my gaze and seemed lost for words.

"In response to your question," I continued, "no, I do not want or need attention. And, actually, it is my *place* to meddle, if I wished to do so, which I don't. Yes, I am an Amory. No, I am not the Amory Ancestor who caused magic to be banned in the Modern World. I am my own person, with my own morals. Time has moved on, four hundred years, in fact. And I would appreciate it if you would talk about me with respect."

The man looked around, and then at Juno. Juno shrugged. He sat back down. I looked at her, trying to engage with her thoughts. The corner of her mouth turned up in a smile. I retook my seat.

Another hand was raised.

"Yes, Ancestor Rutland."

A younger looking lady stood up. I guessed she would have been in her forties when she died. She spoke with a Nigerian accent. "Ancestor Juno, I am so glad to be here. Firstly, I have no problem with the Lunar witches joining us. I welcome it. My question is, will the alteration of the Myst affect us?"

She smiled at me and Asher before looking back at Juno.

"Ancestor Crescent and I have been working hard on the spell that will, if agreed, be used to alter the Myst and welcome lunar magic. Of course, with any spell, these questions cannot be answered with complete certainty. We cannot predict the future, or the outcome of the spell. However, I can assure you that two of the most powerful witches to exist have composed this spell. It will be checked numerous times before use. I also ask you to please remember that if, in an unlikely case, the spell misbehaves, myself and Ancestor Crescent have the ability to reverse it. The Myst is my creation, and I will always find a way to make it a safe and happy place to be," Juno said.

Hands that were previously raised fell and were not raised again. Juno had answered their questions and reassured them of her abilities. They clung to every word she spoke, believing everything she said with a certain confidence that I had never seen before. They trusted her.

"Ancestor Baylen," Juno said.

I knew this name. Ancestor Baylen was the one who gathered the letters and hid them in the time capsule with the real necklace containing Juno's power. He was one of Juno's most trusted allies.

"Your majesty, Juno, it is wonderful to be united here together again. I am interested to hear from both Mr Curator and Miss Amory. I'd like them to inform us all on why they believe this to be a progressive movement for the Myst."

All eyes fell upon Asher. Of course they wanted to hear from the Curator first.

"I believe that welcoming lunar power to the Myst is essential. It isn't fair to exclude a group of supernatural beings from their rightful afterlife. If we get what we want, four hundred years of division could be resolved. I see no negatives to this. The only risk is that the peace you are all used to could be disturbed. But that will only happen if you allow it to be. This could be a very easy transition. And, on top of that, I want it to happen because Brannon wants it to happen. Her heart is so pure. She is the most caring person I have ever met, and I feel honoured to share this pendant with her."

It was pointless, trying to hide my smile because we were in front of all these important people. Asher wasn't hiding his. Juno wasn't even hiding hers! So, I smiled. Because I love him. I'd tell it to the world if I could.

Now, the attention was on me. I let my passion override my nervousness or worry about my surname. It was time to fight my case.

"Okay," I said, sitting on the edge of my seat. "My best friend is gay." Everyone looked around in confusion, clearly wondering how or why this was relevant. "On our first day of secondary school, a group of boys, who were a couple of years older, shoved him against the lockers and called him a 'pretty boy'. The next week, they tripped him over in the corridor and yelled about how he was gay. Everyone laughed. He hadn't officially come out yet, not that it should require a big announcement, but he didn't deny it. He knew he was.

"In our next school year, a group of girls started claiming that they were worried my best friend would steal their boyfriends. The year after that, he was pushed over on the playground and a video of him was sent round the school. No one did anything to make it better for him. I tried, really hard, but it wasn't enough.

"You're probably thinking, why is she telling us this? Why should we care?

"Now, I'm positive that, even if these things didn't occur throughout the entirety of our school lives, that I would still feel this way. But watching my best friend be bullied for being different solidified it for me. I would never watch anyone be discriminated against for simply being different, or simply being. In fact, I'm very passionately against it."

I had the attention of every witch, vampire and werewolf in front of me. They were listening intently.

"Now, this is completely different. But the root of it is similar. People are being treated unfairly for being less powerful than others. When I found out that the Lunar witches don't get to explore their magic like everyone else here, I knew that something needed to be done. I knew that I wouldn't be able to stop until they were treated as equals. Because they deserve to be. Everyone deserves to be.

"My best friend also happens to be a Lunar witch, unbeknown to me until a week ago. His name is Blain Crescent." People gasped at the sound of his surname, realising that he descended from the most powerful Lunar witch to exist. "He is the strongest person I know. The thought of him being excluded, again, from somewhere he has every right to be pains me. The Myst was created as an afterlife for all supernatural beings who do not get the chance to explore their abilities in their lifetime. Lunar witches are supernatural. They should have the opportunity to experience this. And, for those of you that it bothers, you shouldn't be bothered. You shouldn't, really, care. As long as they are kind and respectful to you, as you should be to them, what does it matter?"

I paused, wondering if this was making any difference at all.

"Look," I said, lowering my voice and slowing down, "I was raised by a Sol witch, who I know would have welcomed the Lunar witches into the community willingly, agreeing that their detachment from magic is unfair. I remember my dad saying to me, 'Everyone has a voice, but not everyone is heard. Make sure you're always listening.' Well, this is me listening. And I hope you'll listen, too."

Silence.

I could feel my heart in my throat.

A lady at the back stood up. I didn't have to wonder who she was. I recognised her immediately.

Helena Black. A Lunar witch. And a proud one, too.

Everyone stared at her. She looked at me, and I sensed the feeling of pride.

Confidently, and with no hesitation, she lifted both her hands and started to applaud me. No one joined in but she didn't stop.

People started to turn their heads to look at me. Their gaze transitioned between me and Mrs Black. And, after everything I'd experienced today, what happened next surprised me the most.

An elderly man stood up and started clapping, too. Then another Ancestor, and another, until most of the crowd were applauding me.

I was beyond confused. I looked at Asher. He was beaming with pride. Juno was clapping and smiled at me as if to say, 'I knew you could do it.'

I looked back towards the crowd. Even the man who despised me earlier was clapping for me now.

I didn't know what to do. I smiled whilst wiping a tear from my cheek. They had listened. Everyone had listened.

Asher

Juno held out her hands, instructing everyone to sit back down. The clapping stopped but my smile didn't fade. If anyone could win over this crowd, it would be her. My beautiful Amory.

"Ancestor Baylen, I hope that Mr Curator and Miss Amory's answers were satisfactory," Juno said. A few people chuckled. As if that reaction didn't prove it already. "The Myst is a democracy and, for those of you who cared to join us today, the choice is yours to make."

Silence fell once more. This was the make-or-break moment. The moment that decided the future of the witches.

"Please raise your hand if you oppose the suggested alteration to the Myst," Juno said.

It took a while for someone to raise their hand but after one went up, a couple more followed. I felt frustrated knowing, after hearing what Brannon had to say, that they still didn't want to welcome lunar power to the Myst. But some people are stuck in their ways and are simply not open to changing their mind.

"Very well," Juno said. "Please raise your hand if you are in support of the suggested alteration to the Myst."

This time, hands shot up quicker. It was like a wave, the way hands rose up. It was a sight I was thankful to see.

Brannon looked at me, not even attempting to conceal her happiness. This was a big deal. After four hundred years of this inequality, she had done it. She had put it right.

"Then it is decided," Juno announced, "life for the Lunar witches is about to transform." Juno smiled. "Thank you all, dearly, for gathering here today. I hope you can agree with me that the pendants are in the most deserving hands. I declare the gathering is dismissed."

Juno instructed us to stay in our seats as everyone left. We received many smiles and bows of the head, which I never would have predicted would happen when we first arrived. A few friendly faces waved goodbye and I noticed the lady who stood up first to applaud Brannon mouth 'thank you' to us both. After the chairs were empty, Juno congratulated us and we walked down the beach, towards the sunset.

Brannon

The walk back through the sun was as strange as it was on our way in, but I was too thrilled to care.

I felt as though I had rewritten the future of any and all Amorys to come. I had erased the darkness that hovered over my surname and redirected its history. It was a feeling I rarely felt, but I was proud of myself. And I was proud of Asher, too.

"I must say," Juno said, as our feet hit the sand on the other side, "well done."

"Thank you," I said.

"Means a lot, Juno," Asher said.

"I have to inform Ancestor Selene of the progress. She will be overjoyed. We will need to analyse the spell in detail and figure out what needs to be done to make sure the spell lasts. It shouldn't take us long. I will summon you both again when we are ready, to explain what we discover. Then we will arrange for the spell to be cast," Juno explained.

We both nodded. We said our goodbyes, and Juno walked back through the sun. Although, in my opinion, it was more of a happy stroll.

The sun swallowed her up. I turned to face Asher.

His jaw must have ached from the smile on his face. He didn't say anything. Instead, he picked me up and swung me around. His excitement got the better of him and he forgot how hard he was squeezing me as he jumped up and down, a happiness in him that I hadn't yet seen.

"God, I love you," he said. "I just really love you."

I laughed. "I love you. To the moon and never back."

Asher

When we opened our eyes again, it was night-time. Silvia and Blain were still there, waiting for us.

"Thank goodness," Silvia said, as we came back around. I sat up as she spoke. "I was getting so worried. That was an extremely long episode."

I helped Brannon sit up. I noticed that Silvia and Blain had found blankets to cover their legs.

"Well, if the smile on both of your faces doesn't mean you were successful, I'll be damned," Blain said, holding his hands in the air.

"They agreed," Brannon said. "They're letting lunar power back in!"

"Oh, Brannon," Silvia cried. "Oh, Asher. How can we thank you?"

"No thank you required," I said. "We wanted this, too."

Silvia sprung up and hugged us both, Blain joined in. The rest of the evening was spent with Silvia questioning what it would be like to be in the Myst, with the powers of a Lunar witch.

I took Brannon out the next day, to go paddle boarding. Having watched a recent competition, I felt eager to get back into the sea.

We pushed the boards into the ocean until the water was waist height. Then I helped Brannon to scramble up on top. She tried to be elegant, but it was impossible.

I climbed on behind her and instructed her to stay on her knees or sit down. She had to keep reminding me that she wasn't new to this and if she had a paddle board of her own, she'd be miles ahead of me by now.

I found my balance, standing up I started to use the paddle to push us farther out. I noticed that the weight of two people made it much harder to move at a steady pace, but as the water got deeper, the easier it was. The sea carried us, moving beneath the board and bobbing us up and down gently.

I'd have loved to see Brannon's face, but I found things to love about the back of her. How her hair turned lavender in the sunlight. How it looked so soft and silky as it trailed down her back. The way her shoulders looked smooth and shiny, especially when the sun hit them.

How she sat so still, with complete trust in my ability to keep us both on the board. She didn't flinch when we started to wobble. But maybe that's because the ocean didn't scare her.

I paddled to a point where we could see the beach in the distance but were surrounded by quietness. All I could hear was the water as it moved elegantly around us. There was a breeze, but it couldn't be classed as wind today. It was too gentle.

It felt like we were closer to the sun, now. I could feel the heat on my skin, a scorching temperature today, and made sure to splash water over Brannon's legs and shoulders every now and then.

Slowly and steadily, I lowered myself to sit down. Brannon turned to face me. We both dangled our legs in the water, either side of the board. It cooled us down immediately.

I had decided to take Brannon out to give us both a break. The supernatural world was proving to be intense and there was so much information for us to process and understand. I felt as though I needed a day off from it, and I wanted to take Brannon with me.

"I have one rule," I said, looking into her lilac eyes, "no supernatural talk. For one day."

I don't think she saw the point in it, but she agreed anyway.

"Let's play a game," she said, grinning at me.

The water continued to move us up and down and side to side.

"Okay," I said, "what game?"

"We get three questions each," she said. "Three things you really want to know about the other person. And then you answer them, honestly."

"Sounds like a good game," I said, apprehensive about what she'd ask.

"I'll go first. What did you first notice about me?" Brannon asked.

"Your eyes. I'd never seen eyes quite as beautiful as yours. To be honest, it took me a moment to realise that they meant you were an Amory because I was just lost in them. They caught my attention. And like a fish on a hook, you reeled me in," I said.

Her cheeks turned pink. My words still made her blush.

"Good answer," she said, giggling nervously. "Now it's your turn to ask me."

I had to think for a while. I wanted to ask her the same thing but, knowing Brannon, I guessed that would be against the rules.

"Do you think I give you enough alone time?" I asked.

"Yes, definitely. I mean, I'm alone when you're at work and I enjoy occupying myself. It also gives me a chance to miss you. I know it's only a day, at most, but I love the feeling of being excited to see you. It's important to do your own thing," she said. "But I don't think I would ever get fed up with you."

Her words were heartfelt. We were sitting, alone at sea, in a bubble of complete happiness. I was starting to like this game a lot.

"An equally good answer," I said, winking at her. She loves it when I wink at her.

"Okay, my next question is, do you think you would still love me if I lived in Heston?" she asked.

"Bran, you could be anywhere in the world, and I'd still love you," I said. "If you're asking if I could move on from you if you weren't here, the answers no. It would never happen. Imagine trying to replace you? Impossible. I don't care how many miles apart we are; I'll love you all the same."

"Good," she said, leaning in to kiss my cheek.

"Can I ask you the same thing?" I said.

"Hmm, you're not supposed to. But you can this time," she said. "My answers the same as yours, though. Wherever I am, or wherever you are, you'll always have my heart."

Her answer was short but sweet, and I loved it. She didn't need to say anything else. That was enough.

"Okay, my last question," she said. "When did you realise you loved me?"

I had to think about this one. I can't remember a day when I didn't love her. But she wanted a moment.

"Well, I knew, after I first looked at you, that there would be no turning back. But if I had to say a moment that I knew I was in love with you, it would be on the zipline. It terrified me, and when you let go of the strap and held your arms back, nothing to hold onto if you fell, it was one of the scariest moments of my life. But I saw how happy it made you and realised that it didn't matter how I felt, it mattered how you felt. And that's what love is, really, isn't it? Wanting someone else to be happy."

She listened to every word I spoke, so intently. I noticed the glistening of her eyes.

"Wow," she said, "that was a really good answer."

We laughed, shaking off the seriousness.

"Okay, your last question," she said.

"What's the biggest lesson you've learnt from being with me?" I asked.

"Easy," she said, holding my hands in hers. "I used to see myself as weird. And, I'm sorry for mentioning it, but I couldn't accept the supernatural parts of me. The headaches and the fainting, it was all too strange. I wanted nothing more than a normal life. Until I met you. You took me on adventures, introduced me to escapism and showed me a life that was so far from normal. And I loved it. I loved you. I loved how you made me feel different, and special because of it. Asher, the biggest lesson I've learnt from you is that I don't want normal." She paused, looking directly into my eyes. "I want extraordinary."

This time, I felt my eyes watering.

"I think that's the best answer," I said.

"Good game?" she asked.

I nodded with vigour. "Very good game."

We lost ourselves in each other's smiles for a moment. Then, I found my balance standing up again, and pushed us back through the water, to shore.

We spent the evening with my parents. My mum cooked a Greek style dinner to celebrate our success with Juno.

"I'll hand it to you, Brannon," my dad said. "You've done amazingly."

I knew this meant a lot to her. It meant a lot to me, too.

"I told you, Roger," my mum said, "you needed to have more faith."

Brannon smiled. Mum sipped her wine. Dad tucked into his gyros. I brushed my hand over Brannon's knee under the table. Life was good.

"You two don't realise how big of a deal this is," my dad said. "You will go down in supernatural history. Not just your surnames. You."

I squeezed her knee three times, and she squeezed my hand three times back.

Life was more than good. And Brannon was getting what she wanted.

It's extraordinary.

Brannon

I took Blain to the beach, just me and him for the day. I wanted to spend some quality time with him before he went home, whenever that would be.

We left just before lunch to set up. We managed to find two sun loungers, an umbrella for shade and I brought a cool box to keep some snacks and cans of drink in.

Our day started with some grilled chicken wraps, filled with salad and mayonnaise. They were so tasty, and extremely filling.

Then we sunbathed for an hour. I had to cover Blain in sun cream every twenty minutes to prevent him from turning a tomato red, but I didn't mind. I didn't want to see him burnt again.

Then we fetched my double seated inflatable and took it out on the water. I can imagine it was quite humorous for the people on the beach, watching me and Blain get into the inflatable. We figured we'd have to jump at the same time because it kept tipping one of us out due to it being unbalanced.

There were moments in the day that I genuinely forgot about everything to do with Juno. It had been playing on my mind constantly and I appreciated Asher's efforts to escape it, but I didn't want to. I enjoyed asking myself questions about it and being absorbed in the chaos. But being with Blain stripped it from my mind. I was too caught up in belly hurting laughter with my lifelong best friend to think about anything else.

It brought me back to a little over a year ago, when Blain and I were here, carelessly enjoying ourselves at summer camp. I'd missed him so much it hurt. Being with him again felt like home. And freedom. And youth.

We sipped fizzy drinks whilst floating in the inflatable.

"Isn't it just crazy?" Blain asked. "Everything has changed, but nothing has changed at the same time."

"Here we are, enjoying our day, two best friends who also happen to be witches," I said.

"That doesn't sound right, does it?" he said.

"Not at all."

"What's it been like for you? All these years?" Blain asked.

"A lot," I said. "It was a lot for me to understand as a child. I didn't know why I fainted or saw people at a beach and then got a very bad headache. We went to the doctors, hoping for some pain relief. They put it down to migraines. I've been on medication since I was six. But now I do understand, and it's a lot more. To comprehend why this is the way things are and to think of all the history that no one knows about. I mean, Heston is where it all happened! It's home to the biggest witch population in the world, and we grew up in the midst of it."

"That's mental," Blain said. "I can't imagine how hard it was to not talk about it with anyone."

"I did talk about it, with my dad." I paused, still finding it hard to mention my Dad, especially with Blain, who had known him very well. "He had the pendant before me, you know. He was the best person to talk to about it. But he always enforced the seriousness of keeping it a secret."

"I understand why you had to keep it a secret. It's not like I would've understood anyway," Blain said.

"But, Blain, I can't imagine how it was for you to find out all this information at once. I mean, has it even sunk in yet? That you'll be going to a supernatural afterlife one day?" I asked.

"I'll be honest, I wasn't as surprised as you might think. My nan has always mentioned witches and the name Juno wasn't new to me. I just thought she was a bit crazy. I learnt to ignore her, as bad as that sounds. But when she did tell me, it made sense. As the words said, it started with me. We became best friends, naturally. Then, I was told to pressure you into coming to camp. Then I had to find these objects and hide them around Heston, although it wasn't really hiding them it was just making them easier for you to find. It didn't all hit me at once," he said. "But I don't see myself as a witch. Maybe I will one day, when I'm old and on my way out. Right now, though, I can't do spells or magic or chant in witch language. I'm not important to the supernatural world."

If only Blain knew that it was the story of his strength and courage that won over the Ancestors and persuaded them to accept the Lunar witches again. If only he knew how important he really was.

"I'll get your necklace back to you soon," I said.

"Oh, don't worry. They need it more than I do."

I took his hand in mine and held it.

"I missed you, Blain," I said.

"I missed you, more, Branny."

Asher

I joined Brannon and Blain for pizza at Brannon's cabin after work. I could hear the radio playing and them singing from the front door. I figured that they had enjoyed a great day together.

When I walked into the kitchen they were dancing around the island, using a wooden spoon and a whisk as microphones. I grabbed a spatula and joined in, because why not?

A couple of songs later, we turned the music down and took the pizza bases out of the oven. We spread a generous layer of tomato puree over them, then sprinkled on cheese, chicken and chorizo.

We waited for the cheese to melt, then enjoyed the pizzas. They were delicious.

It made me happy, to see Brannon happy. I know I make her laugh, but this laughter was different. One only a best friend can cause.

She left the kitchen to shower off the sun cream and change into her PJ's.

"She missed you, you know," I said to Blain as he started washing up the dishes. I grabbed a tea-towel and stood next to him.

"I know," he said. "I missed her, too."

"I was really angry at you at one point," I said. "I watched her face drop every time she checked her phone for a message from you."

"Asher, you have no idea how many messages I typed out but didn't send. I wanted to talk to her so bad. I just couldn't."

"I guess it's done now. I'm just glad she has you back."

"I'm glad I have you both back," he said.

We shared a smile, then finished the washing up.

Brannon put a film on for us to watch. She fell asleep within the first half hour. Blain managed another twenty minutes. I covered them with the throw and headed to Brannon's bed.

When I woke up the next morning, her body was cuddled into mine. She had found her way back to me in the night, but I was too much of a deep sleeper for that to have woken me up.

"Good morning," she said, in her delicate morning voice, as she stretched out her arms.

I kissed her on the head. "Morning, gorgeous."

"I hope today is the day," she said.

She never stopped thinking about it.

"What's the plan if it's not?" I asked.

"Blain wants us to spend the day in his cabin, in the garden with Silvia, and have a BBQ later on."

"Sounds good."

Brannon

We hadn't been there long. I was lying beside Asher on beach towels on the grass, reading. He dropped his book and his eyes fluttered as he was summoned away. A buzz of excitement shot through me at the thought of being next to go.

I wondered if Silvia and Blain were fed up with us leaving their company so suddenly, but I knew they wouldn't really mind.

Juno was already waiting and greeted us with a smile, yet I sensed not all was well.

"It's good to see you both," she said, taking our hands and gently squeezing them.

Asher seemed uneasy too. I know he always goes into these things with apprehension. He prepares for bad news. Whereas I can't control myself. I get carried away with the thrill of it all and forget that we are dealing with the supernatural. It's unpredictable and risky. It's unknown.

He ran one of his tanned hands through his walnut coloured ringlets that nested on his head. His eyebrows were thick but well-shaped. I could see them better when he lifted his hair. I watched the apple of his throat move as he swallowed, his jaw looking chiselled as ever. He looked at me with his azure blue eyes, silently checking that I was okay. I was staring at him in admiration. He was the only thing to distract me from everything else. The only exception.

"What news do you have for us?" he asked.

"Yes. Right. Let's get into it, shall we? The spell is complete," Juno said. She hesitated.

"There's a but?" I asked.

"I'm sorry to say, yes. There is a but. It requires certain sacrifices. Not a sacrifice of life, just life as we all know it."

Juno had a way with words. She could usually make something sound so obvious when it was actually really complex. On this occasion she'd only managed to confuse me more. I frowned. "Mmm, what does that mean?"

"Let me explain," Juno said, taking a deep breath. "Performing the spell is the simple part. However, making it last and adjusting the Myst for such a drastic change is where the confusion lies.

"In order to make the spell last, a pendant will need to be present, often, in the Myst. I know this is far from ideal, but it is the only way."

I didn't know what to think of it.

"So me or Brannon will have to…what?…live in the Myst?" Asher asked.

Juno looked at both of us, her gaze more serious than I'd ever seen.

"I'm afraid so. You will be able to leave whenever you wish, but you will have to return daily to ensure that the spell is functioning properly and you will not be able to be gone for too long. I also believe that whoever takes this role will be able to help me rule over the Myst, and ensure the continuation of peace."

I could sense Asher's sadness. He couldn't bear the thought of being without me. But I didn't see it like that. We wouldn't be without each other. We could see each other whenever we liked. But one of us would have to base our lives in the Myst, whilst the other lived at camp.

The thought of ruling over the Myst with Juno excited me. It was an opportunity that I would love to take. But I needed to talk to Asher, away from Juno. "We'll need time to think about this," I said.

"Yes, of course. I do not expect you both to make that decision right now. It will require, I'm sure, an in-depth conversation to discuss the complexities of this. If it so happens that neither of you are willing to take on this duty, that is understandable. However, the spell will not work. The magic of the Myst is linked to these pendants. This spell will, therefore, be linked to the pendants too. The active magic in the pendants will need to be present in the Myst to ensure the proper functioning of the spell. Like me. I have to be in the Myst to ensure that it functions.

"Is that it?" Asher asked.

"Not quite. I'm afraid that there is an additional problem. The Myst needs to be anchored by two external pendant holders. If one of you chooses to join me in the Myst they will not be able to continue as an anchor as well. We will need to introduce another holder.

"The Crescent necklace will continue to be used to withhold lunar power. We have decided to also grant it the power of an anchor. Ideally, a Lunar witch will need to do this, but we can work out the finer details of that later. Does that make sense?" Juno asked, looking to me.

"Yes," I said.

Asher didn't answer. I held his hand, but he was reluctant to hold it back. It wasn't my fault this was happening. Or was it?

"Mr Curator?" Juno asked.

He nodded but looked at the floor.

"I'm going to leave you both to discuss this information," Juno said. "Please return tomorrow. Midday. We will talk about your decisions."

"Bye, Juno," I said.

Asher said nothing.

Asher

We opened our eyes again. I stretched my neck, then stood up.

Silvia and Blain were waiting with smiling faces for what we had to say. I wasn't in the mood.

"Me and Brannon need to talk," I said.

Their smiles faded but they didn't question it. I walked back through the cabin and out the front door. Brannon followed behind me.

I looked into the future. I saw myself alone. This wasn't going to end well.

We got to the pier but neither of us sat down. We stood there, arms crossed, looking at each other.

"What's your problem?" Brannon asked. I could hear the attitude in her tone.

I shook my head, unable to put my feelings into words.

"Well?" she said. "You said we needed to talk. Let's talk."

"Fine," I said. "I don't know if I can go through with it."

"What do you mean?" she asked.

"The spell," I said. "It means one of us has to live in the Myst, without the other."

"We can still see each other," she said.

"That's not the point. It will be different."

"How?" she asked.

"Because, Brannon, one of us will have duties that will curtail us. Our time together will be limited because the Myst will need one of us more. We'll be living completely different lives. I know you want an extraordinary life, but this is too far. This is too far from normal."

"Asher, you know how much this means to me," she said, anger and disappointment pushing her to the edge. "It wouldn't be as bad as you think. One of us would live there, yes, but we can come back sometimes."

"You wouldn't though, would you?" I said, raising my voice and instantly regretting it.

She took a step back. A wave crashed violently into the pier.

"You're assuming I'd be the one to go?"

"I know you would be, Brannon. I know you'd want to."

She looked around, probably figuring out if this was a good moment to admit that I was right.

"Well, yeah, if we're being honest, I do want to. I feel like I don't have a purpose right now. You have camp. You have a life planned out. Did you seriously think I'd be able to live my entire life like this? I can't. I've found something that I'm passionate about and it's the supernatural world."

"Exactly, so you're going to leave me," I said.

"I'm not going to do anything unless we both agree. But if one of us has to go, then I will. I don't see the problem with it, Asher."

"The problem is that I don't want things to change. We wanted to change the Myst, not for it to change our entire lives!" I said, the volume of my words increasing.

"Change isn't a bad thing," she said, raising her voice to a level to match mine. "You're so used to being my only priority that you're scared I'll get distracted and forget about you."

She could read me like a book.

"I just don't want to lose what we have. It's too big of a risk."

She looked at the floor. "I can't let the Lunar witches down now," she said. "I'm sorry, Asher. This has to be done."

She didn't look at me as she turned around and walked off. Away from me.

Brannon

I sat on my sofa, head in my hands, and finally let it all out. Every overwhelming emotion that I didn't realise had been weighing me down.

Tears spilled and I lost control of my breathing. My chest tightened and my eyes stung. But my head cleared as the emotions poured out of me. I could think straight, at least.

Juno was right, it wasn't ideal. We didn't expect this as the outcome. We thought that the Myst would change and our lives would be untouched. But that was naïve. We were naïve.

In my opinion, it would work out fine. We wouldn't spend as much time together, but why was that such a bad thing? I would feel useful in the Myst, helping Juno to keep peace and diving headfirst into the supernatural world. I would see Asher whenever he wasn't working. He forgets he has camp to keep him busy. We could do the things we do now, when we are both free. It would surely make us appreciate our time together even more.

Juno hadn't clarified. Maybe it wouldn't be forever. It might take a few years for the Myst to accept this change. After all, it would be a big change. For everyone. Even Juno. The first job was welcoming back lunar power, but that's the easy part. She'd then have to unite the witches and gain their respect after acting so heartlessly towards them all those years ago. I could help her with that. Explain how everyone makes mistakes. Help Juno to tell them her side of the story and earn her forgiveness.

Juno could help me, too. She could teach me how to develop my powers and strengthen them. I could bring this guidance back to Asher and help him, too. Although I sensed he didn't want this.

When I met him, it was clear that he and his father had studied the supernatural world. Asher knew my history before I did. He was taught about the past and the reason we had these pendants, whereas I had no idea. My dad tried to keep me from it. He wanted me to have a normal childhood. I think that was the right move because I would have felt constantly stressed with the severe headaches as well as trying to remember everything from the history books. It would've overwhelmed me and fogged up my innocent, clear mind with constant thoughts and questions. I'd know I was being punished for what the bad Ancestor did. It could've made me hate the world. It could've made me hate myself, working as a self-fulfilling prophecy.

The difference between me and Asher used to be that he was deeper into the supernatural world than I was. I was an amateur. A new starter. A beginner. I felt as though I didn't have a right to be involved in it like he was. I didn't feel as though it was my place. But I was naturally pulled into it. I fell in love and kept the pendant. I went on a supernatural treasure hunt around Heston. I read letters from witches. I studied book after book and listened as people explained the history of the Myst to me. Unintentionally, I got myself involved. I learnt everything I could and did anything I could to help.

I discovered that it didn't scare me. I wasn't intimidated by the facts or put off by the history. I gained confidence in doing these things and felt like I learnt just as much about myself. For the first time in my life, I felt like I belonged. Like I was meant to be there. In the midst of it all.

Asher didn't share my enthusiasm or interest. He was content with his everyday life. It was enough for him to survive like everyone else, with a lot of spontaneous adventures along the way. His life isn't normal. Neither is our love story. But I've said before that being with him offered me a balance between reality and the supernatural world, and I used to appreciate that. I still did.

He didn't throw himself in quite as deeply as me. He learned what he had to and was satisfied with that. There's nothing wrong with that. But I knew he wasn't enjoying how intense this part of our journey had been. He didn't feel comfortable walking to our chairs in front of the Ancestors. He didn't enjoy the feeling of venturing in and out of the Myst. He didn't find excitement or opportunity in what Juno had to say.

I understood his reservations. He was scared I would forget him. Get too caught up in a new life. But I knew I wouldn't. He meant more than anything to me, and if he really didn't want me to do this, then I wouldn't. But he was the one that said love is wanting to make someone else happy.

This would make me happy.

Asher

Slamming my bedroom door shut, I curled up on my bed, resting my head on my pillow, already feeling lost without her.

Maybe I relied on her too much. I should be able to provide myself with happiness, but she was better at it.

She changed my life when I met her. My life was never bad, but it wasn't amazing. She brought a new energy that I had never felt before and taught me how to love. She showed me a happier side to life that I'll never be ready to let go of.

I felt pathetic. I knew I was in the wrong. She wasn't leaving me or neglecting me or abandoning me. She wanted to do this for the Lunar witches. She wanted to make things right for them, and so did I. I pushed for this like she did. But the thought of her forgetting about me and her life here scared me. Everything was perfect. But she was right. I couldn't expect her to live like this forever. She needed to feel like she had a purpose.

And she'd found her purpose. I just couldn't accept the consequences of it. I wouldn't be able to turn up at her door whenever I liked, because she might not be there. I couldn't expect her to be sleeping beside me every night, because she might be busy dealing with something else. She might be needed in the Myst. Without me.

But she would be able to come and see me. We could arrange the days and times. She could escape some nights and cuddle with me in bed. We could still go to the lagoon and climb into the small boats. We could watch the sunset, if she wasn't sick of them, which I don't think she ever would be. We could spend time in the town, eating too much food. We could have bonfires and beach days and BBQs and evenings in the hot tub. Our life would change, but perhaps it could work.

I felt angry at myself. I'd upset her. Made her believe that I was willing to let her down. And for what? If I'd just taken a few minutes to think about this properly, then I'd have realised we would be fine. I wouldn't have raised my voice and she wouldn't have walked away. How it pains me to watch her walk away.

This was pointless and selfish of me. I asked her, when we were paddle boarding, if she would love me even if we weren't close together. She told me that no matter where we both were, I'd always have her heart.

And she'd have mine, too. Always and forever. I'd been an idiot.

Brannon

We spent the night apart. I didn't hear from him, and he didn't hear from me. I fell asleep on my sofa, tears dripping down my face. It was probably for the best.

When I woke, I was feeling better. The intense emotions had dissolved, and I was ready to talk. I showered and changed into a white dress with a strappy back. One of his favourites.

I was about to message him to come over when there was a knock on my door. I opened it to find him standing there, arms crossed, shoulder leaning against the wall.

"Morning," I said.

"I'm sorry," he said.

Asher didn't struggle with apologies. He was the first to say sorry, and he always meant it.

He walked in and sat on a stool at the kitchen island. I stood opposite. I watched him look me up and down, trying to conceal a smile.

"What?" I asked.

"You're gorgeous," he said.

One look into his ocean eyes was enough to melt away my anger.

"So, where's your head at?" I asked.

"I feel bad," he said. "I was selfish and only thinking about myself. But I spent last night thinking about you, and how it would be good for you to have your own project, like I have camp. I think I was just scared, but I should've known better. I can't keep you to myself forever. Juno would be lucky to have you as her partner."

My heart burst. I half suspected we would have another disagreement but by the sound of things we weren't going to. We weren't on the same page, exactly. But it sounded like we were at least on the same chapter.

"Asher, you have no idea how much that means to me," I said, hugging him around the waist. "I will be yours forever. And I'm not going to stop loving you, ever, no matter where I am. I'll always come back to see you."

I felt his arms around my back, pulling me in to him.

"I love you, Bran," he said.

"I love you, Ash."

We hugged for a while longer. Disagreeing with each other wasn't a bad thing. It never is. As long as we both remember that our love is worth more than whatever it is we're disagreeing over, then we'd be fine. Our love is always worth more than the fight.

"So," he said, "Juno's looking for another pendant holder. How're you feeling about that?"

"I didn't like the idea of it at first. But then I had an idea."

He looked at me, suspiciously. "Go on," he said.

"Well, Juno said the new owner of the Crescent necklace should be a Lunar witch. I was thinking that, really, there's no one better for the job than Blain. His nan can help him if he needs it. You get along with him, so you wouldn't have to meet a stranger. He would be very good at comforting people in death. And we know, for a fact, we can trust him."

Asher nodded as I spoke. "I can't believe I didn't think of it myself. Do you think Blain will want to, though?"

I'd thought about it from his perspective. He had embraced the supernatural life as soon as he discovered it. He had a lot of knowledge already from his nan and the objects. He'd be open to learn, and Asher and I could guide him through it. We could tell him what we already know.

"I think he would," I said.

"Well, let's go suggest the idea to him."

I put my sliders on, ready to walk over to Blain's cabin. Asher stopped me as I opened the door.

"Brannon," he said, "I really am sorry."

I leant in and kissed his lips.

"No more apologies," I said, taking his hand and leading the way to Blain's.

Silvia and Blain must've worried all night. Asher had made us leave so abruptly yesterday, with no explanation of what had happened in our last visit to the Myst.

"Please tell me you haven't come here to announce a breakup," Blain said as he opened the door.

I laughed. "Don't be silly."

He walked us through to the garden, where Silvia was sitting on a wicker chair enjoying a cup of morning coffee.

"Oh, Brannon," she said, with a smile, "I'm glad you're here. And you Asher. We were so confused."

"That's my bad, Silvia. I wasn't pleased with the news Juno delivered to us. I had to talk to Brannon, as a matter of urgency," Asher said.

"Take a seat," Silvia said. "Let's talk about it."

When Blain had fetched us each a glass of orange and mango juice with ice, we relayed the facts as we knew them. Once we'd finished, there was a brief silence until Silvia spoke up.

"I hope you don't mind me asking, but have you decided which one of you it will be that stays in the Myst?"

"Yes, it will more than likely be me," I said.

"If Brannon didn't want to, then I would have done it. I'm aware of how much she's sacrificed already to be with me and would completely understand if she didn't want to give up any more of her life. But she doesn't see it that way," Asher said.

I think he assumed they would judge him for not stepping up so felt the need to explain himself. Whilst it was unnecessary, it was nice to hear. It was nice to know he would have taken on the role if I was against it, to see out something that I pushed for in the first place.

"I enjoy being involved in the supernatural," I said. "I would love to experience it and assist Juno over there."

Silvia's smile was enthusiastic and proud.

"Juno also told us that another pendant holder will need to be recruited. She has decided to use the Crescent necklace as the third pendant. It makes sense. The first two make a sun, this one is a moon. She said she would like a Lunar witch to become an anchor for the Myst too. The Myst is powered by our pendants, so I think the necklace will work as a powerhouse for lunar magic," Asher said.

"So, I was thinking," I said, "Who do we know who is not only a Lunar witch but also incredibly brave, full of strength and compassion, and would fit in with me and Asher extremely well?"

I made eye contact with Blain.

"Me?" he asked, his voice almost shrill with shock.

"Oh, this is wonderful!" Silvia said. "You have to accept, Blain. The Amory's, Curator's and Crescents have always been linked. You three can pick up where they left off!"

Poor Blain didn't even have time to think it through, we were meeting with Juno in a few hours and I wanted to suggest my idea to her, before she found someone else for the job.

"I don't know," Blain said. "I don't know if I'll be good at it."

"Neither did Asher or I when we were assigned this role at birth, but you learn. You'll be a pro in no time," I said.

"Come on, Blain. We'd all make a great team," Asher said.

Blain rolled his eyes and smiled. "Fine," he said.

His agreement was followed by a round of applause from Silvia.

"But, just so you know, I'm terrified at the prospect," he added.

"We'll guide you through it all," Asher said.

"I wouldn't ask if I wasn't sure," I said.

Silvia decided we had to celebrate whilst we were still here, despite the fact that nothing was official yet. She made sandwiches and poured us all a glass of Prosecco that she had brought from one of the shops.

The pressure was now on to convince Juno that this was a good idea, although I couldn't see why she would object.

The clock moved towards noon fast, and it was soon time for me and Asher to revisit the Myst. Blain joined us as we walked to the beach. He wanted to analyse what happened when we fell into an episode, in case he would have to do it, too. Then we shut our eyes and escaped reality. My favourite thing to do.

Asher

This time we arrived before Juno, but I could see her walking through the water towards us.

"Are you sure about this, Brannon?" I asked.

"I am," she said, a genuine smile on her face.

Juno wore her black cloak again. I took another guess at why she wore it and wondered if it was to disguise herself in the crowds.

"Good afternoon Mr Curator, Miss Amory," she said. "Now, do you have an answer for me?"

Obviously we were past the point of small talk. It seemed now, when we came here we got straight to the point.

"We do," I said.

"I would like to be the one to join you in the Myst," Brannon offered.

"I thought as much," Juno said with a small laugh.

"Also," Brannon continued, "I think Blain, my best friend, should be the new pendant or necklace holder, whatever we are calling them."

"Okay," Juno said, but Brannon didn't seem to hear her and continued to press her point.

"He's not just a Lunar witch, he's descended from Ancestor Selene Crescent. He's been through so much in his life. He's admirable and respectable and so strong and—"

"Miss Amory, I said okay," Juno repeated.

"Oh," Brannon said. "Sorry. It's just, you don't know him. I thought you'd want a description of some sort."

"I trust you, Miss Amory."

Brannon's cheeks reddened. She and Juno had always had a strange relationship. One minute, Brannon was frustrated at her and made no effort to hide it. Next minute, it was as if she respected her opinion more than anyone in the world.

"I will need to meet him," Juno said.

"That's impossible," I said. "You're here and until he's a pendant holder, he's in the living world."

She handed the Crescent necklace to Brannon.

"If you would kindly go back and fetch him? Tell him to put this around his neck and instruct him on how to send your mind here."

Brannon disappeared. It was strange. I'd never seen anyone leave the Myst before, not without me following seconds later. It wasn't sudden. It was as if her body slowly became transparent. Like a wisp of fog being blown by a breeze.

"The necklace has been charged with a lot of lunar magic. Ancestor Selene is a rather powerful witch, if I do say so myself," Juno said. "The necklace has the power to transport Mr Crescent here. He will not have his own powers like the original pendant holders. He will only be able to do what you and Brannon could do before."

"Will Blain have episodes and headaches?" I asked.

"Episodes, yes, which he should manage well considering he has watched Miss Amory have them her entire life. The head aches, no, I shouldn't think so. He has not been cursed like Miss Amory. And, Mr Curator, your headaches are due to the power I had to put inside you, and the spell I did to save your family. That was the consequence. As for Mr Crescent, he will probably not experience them."

"He'll be glad," I said, laughing awkwardly.

I couldn't think of anything else to ask. I'd never had to make conversation with Juno on my own before. It was becoming uncomfortable. I looked around. Juno continued to stare at me, hands joined behind her back.

Hurry up, Brannon.

Brannon

I sat up immediately, trying to ignore the stabbing sensation in my skull.

"Don't freak out," I said, "but you're coming back with me."

"What?!"

"You need to put your necklace back on. I'm assuming it's been laced with magic, now. You're officially an anchor. Juno needs to talk to you as well, so let's go," I said.

Blain looked panicked, but he was speechless. He didn't ask a million questions or refuse. Instead, he reached out, took the necklace and put it on.

"Okay, lay down next to me."

He got into position, and I held his hand.

"Now, close your eyes. You can touch the necklace if it helps. You need to imagine the magic running through your veins. Now focus and listen to my voice. When you feel a sensation pulling on your mind, don't worry. Just let it happen. And remember, you'll be fine. I'll be right behind you. I want you to breathe deeply and see in your mind, a beautiful sunset, sinking over a perfectly still sea on the horizon. The sun is more orange than yellow, and the sky is crimson. The sand is white. And Asher is there."

I could tell he was worried but each word I spoke calmed him. I repeated the description and willed him to see the beach in the Myst. I could tell he had gone when his eyes stopped fluttering and he lay still, his eyes fully shut.

I intertwined my other hand in Asher's. Back between my best friend and him. I used to wonder if it was too soon to call it home, but I'm sure now. This is the closest I felt to home.

Asher

Blain appeared, looking like he was about to have a meltdown.

"Are you okay?" I asked.

"I can't believe what just happened," he said, looking around frantically. "Wow, it's gorgeous. You two never told me how gorgeous it was."

"It truly is," Juno said, greeting him with a smile.

"I'm sorry," Blain said politely, "You are?"

I smacked the palm of my hand against my head. "This is Juno, Blain. Queen of the Heavens," I said.

"Oh, my goodness, I do apologise," he said, bending into an awkward curtsey. I chuckled under my breath.

"What a pleasure it is to meet you, Mr Crescent," Juno said, holding a hand out for him to shake. "It is my honour to welcome you to the Myst. I must thank you, deeply, for accepting this role as your own. I'm sure you will find it most simple in a short while and embrace it to the fullest. Oh, I should inform you. You will only see Lunar witches into the Myst. Your necklace is not quite as powerful as the pendants. You can only accommodate witches like yourself.

"I have much faith in Miss Amory, and I am confident she will have made the right decision in choosing you. Oh, and speaking of Miss Amory, here she is."

As Juno watched Brannon walk over to us, I turned my head to Blain, long enough to see him mouth 'what the hell' at me.

"Now that we are all here, I shall inform you of the plan," Juno said.

We stood in a circle, eager to her what had been decided.

"The spell will happen the day after tomorrow. Your birthdays, I believe?"

Brannon looked at me, mirroring my surprise. Amongst the chaos, we hadn't even realised our birthdays were that soon.

"Please join me at sunset. All three of you. First, I will assess and correct the abilities of the pendants and necklace to ensure they are in perfect condition to move forward. I will award you with your new titles, which Ancestor Selene and I have decided must remain secret until the correct time. We shall designate your roles in a short, private ceremony. Then, we will chant the words and watch as the Myst transforms into a different place. Do you all understand?"

We nodded, and my excitement returned.

"Wonderful. Now, I must leave. Ancestor Selene and I will need to memorise the spell and that will take us the rest of the time we have spare. We cannot read the words from a book. This is old and ancient magic and must be spoken fresh from the mind, straight from the heart. I must admit, but only between the four of us here, I had forgotten how much I enjoyed Ancestor Selene's company," Juno chucked, before turning away. "Oh, one final word," she said, turning to face us again. "Miss Amory, use these last days to say goodbye to your old life. You will be escorting me back into the Myst after the spell is complete, to begin your new journey."

The excitement I had enjoyed, disappeared. And that's when I learnt how it really felt.

Heartbreak.

Brannon

Asher was quiet as we explained what had just happened to Silvia. He was oozing with sadness. He didn't want to lose me to a new life, like Juno had said. But I knew he didn't have to worry. He's my past, present and future. Wherever life takes me, it will never take me from him.

"I am so proud of you three," Silvia said. "We must celebrate some more. How about champagne this time?"

She left to fetch another bottle of drink.

I turned to Asher. "Can I ask a favour?"

"Anything," he said, forcing a smile.

"Do you think your dad could arrange to fly Mum and Marley out for a couple of days?"

"Oh my God," he said, "Brannon, I hadn't even thought about your mum or Marley."

His sadness was replaced by guilt.

"Don't worry, it's fine," I said. "I just want to see them before I go."

"Brannon, maybe you shouldn't be the one to go. You won't get to see them," Asher said, panicking.

"Asher," I said, taking his hands, "I have thought this through. When they visit, they can have my cabin. I will come out and spend time with them during the day, and head back at night. Mum knows not to ask questions. She's taught herself not to for years, ever since she met my dad. Besides, it's not like I see them often anyway."

"And when they are at home in Heston, I will be there to check in on them, as the son she didn't give birth to," Blain said.

I smiled at Blain. Asher stood up. "I'll go arrange their flights now."

"Thank you. I'll ring mum and let her know she's got to come here for a couple of days. I'll say it's an emergency, but not to panic," I said.

"She's going to panic," Blain said.

"Oh, there'll be a lot of panic," I said. We laughed.

I went back to my cabin to ring mum. She was concerned but overjoyed that Roger had paid for and arranged her flights so she and Marley could come visit me here. She hung up the phone, saying that she had best get packing.

I laid back on my bed. My life was about to transform. I'd have one foot here, in my normal life. And one foot, a considerably bigger one, in the supernatural world, my new life. I wondered if I should be feeling nervous, or fearful. Because I wasn't. I felt excited. I couldn't wait to see what my next adventure would entail.

Asher

Celia and Marley's coach arrived at camp in the late afternoon the next day. Marley leapt down the last step and legged it to Brannon, jumping into her arms. She spun him around, squeezing him into her.

Celia did a speed walk over, a beaming grin on her face, and threw her arms around them both. She had her children back together, in the same place. Her smile proved how happy she was.

"We've missed you so much, Bran," Celia said, dragging her suitcase behind her as we walked to Brannon's cabin.

"I've missed you guys, too," Brannon said, holding Marley in her arms.

Marley had so much to tell her. "On Wednesday I was on green face for doing good handwriting but on Thursday I was on silver face!" he said.

"Wow," Brannon said. "Silver face! How did you manage that?"

"Because," Marley said, struggling to get the words out quick enough, "I tidied up the whole classroom and Mrs Leak said it was very good job."

"That's amazing Marley, I'm so proud of you!"

"Marley, why don't you tell Branny about Friday, when you were on red face?" Celia said, sarcastically.

She stared into Marley's eyes, and he shot her a guilty, apologetic look. When she looked away, he looked at Brannon and they silently giggled.

We got back to the cabin, and I took the suitcase to Brannon's room, where they'd be sleeping.

"Brannon, I forget how amazing your life is," Celia said, looking around the kitchen.

"Asher and I have just finished working on the garden. Marley, put your swimming trunks on. Let's sit outside," Brannon said.

Marley swam around the pool, talking to invisible people. Brannon fetched a jug of water for us all, and we sat down to talk.

"Brannon," Celia said, "I've been quite worried, to be honest. Why are we here?"

"It's nothing to worry about," Brannon said. "I know you do a good job staying out of this stuff, and I want you to keep doing that, but it's to do with the pendants."

Celia's face dropped. It was obvious that she wasn't comfortable with this. Used to it, yes. But not comfortable.

"What is it?" Celia asked, her voice a little shaky with worry.

"To put it in a simple way, when I have my episodes, I go somewhere. I'm going to be staying there a lot more," Brannon said.

"I don't like the sound of this," Celia said, shaking her head.

"I didn't either," I said, "but Brannon is amazing at this sort of stuff. You'll have nothing to worry about."

"How will I see you?" Celia asked Brannon.

I could tell from the tone in her voice that she wasn't over the moon about this news. She wasn't comfortable with it, in the slightest. But she also didn't sound as though she was about to refuse it. It sounded like she was used to this. Having to unwillingly accept something.

"Whenever you come here to visit. I can leave when I need to," Brannon said.

Celia seemed to calm down knowing that her daughter wasn't being taken from her.

"Will you come home sometimes, too?" Celia asked.

Brannon

It took me a moment to realise that home meant Heston in this question.

"It will be harder," I said. "When I am in my other life, let's call it, my body will be laid on my bed, here. I can still travel to Heston, but I won't be able to spend all of my time with you as I'll have priorities elsewhere. It would be easier if you came here, which Roger has already said will be no problem."

Me and Asher had agreed to this already. My body would be laid peacefully on my bed. This way, Asher could check on me every day, if he wanted to, and they'd always know where I was.

Mum didn't answer. She was lost in thought, so I gave her a moment.

"I guess I don't really have a choice in the matter," she said. "This wouldn't be the life I'd choose for you. You're going to miss out."

"If I felt like I was going to miss out, I wouldn't take the offer. I think I'll enjoy it more, to be honest. I'll feel like I'm finally somewhere I belong," I said. I took her hands in mine. "Mum, when I moved here to live with Asher, I'm sure that wouldn't have been your first choice for me." She shook her head. "But look how happy I am. You have to trust me. I'll be alright."

She looked at Asher. "And you're on board with this?"

"I wasn't," he said, honestly, "but I know it will make Brannon happy. I hate the thought of things changing, but I guess you'll just have to teach me how to cope with missing her."

He smiled at her, and my mum finally smiled back.

"Oh, Asher," she said, and I could hear that she was about to cry, "there's no way to cope."

Asher smiled, but I don't think my mum's words helped.

"Okay," she said, "you're old enough and mature enough to decide for yourself. I want updates. A lot of updates. I need you to promise that you won't forget about real life. Don't you go forgetting that we're here. You have to visit us."

"Of course I will, Mum." I hugged her.

"I'm not going to tell Marley," she said. "He won't understand, and he'll have so many questions. He won't notice any difference if I don't tell him. Not yet, anyway."

"Okay," I said.

No more was said about it. It took mum a while to adjust to normal again, but she eventually returned to her usual self, happy to be with me again.

Asher's mum invited my family round for tea. I was reluctant, knowing that my mum had already been hit with strong news today, she might not handle it very well if Roger started talking about anything supernatural.

Asher promised his dad wouldn't mention anything considered inappropriate, so I agreed. Roger did a good job of monitoring his supernatural conversations last time they were here. I'm sure he'd do the same again.

The gathering was to celebrate our birthdays. Time had flown past since our exploration of the Lunar witches began. Ageing a year didn't feel like a big deal. The day was now a reminder of when my life changed. When Asher and I chose love. Now, it would mark the day I would leave reality and start a life in the Myst.

Tammy prepared a lovely meal, and the discussions were light and easy. It was great to have everyone together, getting along how they did.

Marley, who got bored quickly, wanted to go to the camps 'kids club' to watch the evening entertainment. I took him down there and watched him throw moves on the dance floor. Then we joined in with a later game of bingo, where we won some magnets and a teddy bear, with Greece written in the same blue letters that were on Silvia's purchases from town. Marley had fun and I appreciated every moment I spent with him. I found myself wondering how much bigger he'd be the next time I saw him and, sometimes, a tear surfaced in my eye. I pushed this thought to the back of my mind. He was probably the only person who could convince me not to do this, and I didn't want convincing.

We got back to Asher's house to find Tammy showing our mum pictures of me and Asher from the last year. We joined them in the lounge.

There were pictures of us on the beach, swimming in the sea. There was another one of us in the hot tub, sipping drink from a champagne glass. Another one showed us in the garden, a shovel in Asher's hand and a pot of flowers in mine. Mum loved looking through them and seeing how happy I truly had been here.

They put the photos away and mum thanked them for a lovely night.

"I'll be off now, got to get Marley to bed," she said, hugging Tammy.

I walked them back to my cabin. They went to bed whilst Asher and I slept on the sofa.

I told him I didn't expect him to sleep on the sofa with me when he had a bed at home, but I don't think he wanted to leave me.

We stayed awake until midnight. When the clock struck twelve and the date on our phones changed to the 4th of July, we shared a kiss.

"Happy birthday, Brannon. Thank you for changing my life."

"Happy birthday, Asher. Thank you for changing mine, too."

Then we cuddled into a corner of the sofa, under blankets, and sunk into the cushions. It was one of the best sleeps I'd had for days.

Asher

I left soon after we woke up, to see my parents. They'd put up a 'happy birthday' banner and lit some candles on a cake. My mum kept saying how she couldn't believe her son was nineteen. Dad kept reminding me that in one year, I'd be the official owner of camp.

They watched me open cards from family and presents from them. They gifted me an electric scooter for myself, and a picture frame that could display twelve pictures. They filled them all with photos of me and Brannon. Then we hung it on my bedroom wall.

I got back to Brannon's cabin moments after they'd finished opening presents, too. Celia had bought her many things, including candles, perfume and a ring with her birthstone in it. I thought it was beautiful. Marley had given her a handmade card, with a picture of him and Brannon holding hands as stick figures.

Celia kindly gave me a new T-shirt with a Cornish surfing brand on it, and a card from Aunt Pat back in Heston.

Then Brannon and I exchanged presents. They were last-minute gifts considering we'd forgotten it was our birthday. I gave her a new paddle board, so that she could have one of her own. She gave me a leather banded bracelet, with the symbol of our pendants engraved on a small silver plaque that rested on the top of my wrist. She'd gone into town quickly yesterday, just before the family meal, and had it hand made at one of the souvenir stores.

"Now we have matching necklaces and bracelets," she said.

It was perfect.

After this, Brannon went to the local food shop to get some more orange juice.

"Celia, I hope you don't mind. I was hoping to spend the day with Brannon," I said.

"Of course!" Celia said.

"I'm going to arrange for everyone to meet at the beach, just before sunset, to say goodbye before she goes. I know we can see her again, but it's so unknown. I don't know how it will work so I thought she would appreciate us seeing her off," I said.

"Oh, that sounds like a wonderful idea, Asher," Celia said. "I'm glad she's loved so much by you."

I took this as a big compliment. I wanted her mum to see how much I love and adore her daughter. How I'd do anything to see her smile.

Brannon laid out Bischoff-spread filled croissants, Pano chocolates and a bowl of freshly cut strawberries and apples in yoghurt. After breakfast, I told her that her mum was happy for me to take her out today. "Put some trainers on," I said. "We're going for a walk."

"Where are we going?" she asked as we passed the semi-crowded beach.

"The first place we ever did," I said. "I mean, technically, the first place we walked was to get more wood for the bonfire. But the first proper path we hiked together was up the mountain, right to the top to see the view."

She smiled.

Brannon

It warmed my heart to know that Asher had thought about this and wanted to take me back to the place where it had all started. The day I had an episode in front of him. The day that our secrets became pointless.

We reached our legs over the stinging nettles. I never did get round to weeding this walk.

Asher gripped my hand the whole way up, as if letting go meant I'd tumble to the bottom. As if it meant I'd disappear into the Myst, and it wasn't time for that yet.

Pretty pink flowers were blossoming amongst the grass and trees on either side of the pathway. When there was a gap between the trees, I noticed how we were progressively getting higher, and I could see the turquoise water and golden sands. This was the best place on Earth.

Time flew by as I embraced every step and appreciated every sight that I saw up the mountain. I didn't know when I'd see it again.

"Do you remember what you asked me on this walk?" Asher said.

"No, what?"

"What did I think happened after death."

We laughed. Subtlety wasn't my gift.

"That was so forward," I said, chuckling.

"I think it was at that point that I realised I liked you. Straight to the point, with the ability to shut me up," Asher said.

But I didn't want to shut him up for the rest of the day. We spoke about our favourite memories together, all the way up the mountain. Like when I told Asher he would be speechless at the sight of a sunset, and he's not been able to prove me wrong yet. And how Asher wouldn't let go of the zipline for even one second when we were flying over camp. Or when Asher tried to not speak to me at the beach one night because his dad advised him that this doesn't have to be a love story. Yet here we are. Completely in love.

Asher

We reminisced on when I screwed up and Blain helped me lay out a picnic on the pier to make it up to Brannon. Or when I had to leave the basement party before I punched a boy in the face for being inappropriate to Brannon.

One memory was my favourite. The moment she opened the door and I saw her. A gorgeous blue gown on her body. Her beautiful purple hair, streaked with silver curls. The night of the summer ball. I'd never thought of humans as art before, until that night. She was a painting; the artist had used their most expensive paints, the most fitting colours, the gentlest hand in creation.

And then we danced. I held her close to me, our bodies moving together to the slow rhythm of the music. I remembered feeling her head delicately rest on my chest, and her hand fit perfectly in mine. I remembered feeling, that night, as though life couldn't get better than this.

The final moment we talked about was our birthdays last year. Not only had we turned eighteen, we'd pledged our loyalty to the Myst, and to each other. I remembered watching the sunset, feeling defeated by life, on the pier. I spoke to the sea, expressing the anger I felt towards myself, and the complete devastation I had about not being with Brannon. But then I remembered hearing her footsteps and the exact words she said. *'Well then, it's a good job I'm keeping the pendant.'* The words that restored happiness in my life. The words that acted as a promise, to each other, that our love would always be enough.

Finally, we reached the top of the mountain. She stood at the edge, watching the world beneath us. I stood behind her, wrapped my arms around her stomach and leant my head on her shoulder.

"Thank you," she said.

"For what?" I asked.

"Everything."

Her voice sounded fragile, as if it could break any minute now.

"I wish there were enough words to tell you how much I love you," I said.

"There aren't," she said, "I've already looked."

I held her tighter.

"You've completed me," I said.

She turned around, her pendant between her fingers. She took mine with her other hand and held them together.

"We complete each other," she said.

After an hour of admiring the view and, more so, each other, we started the walk down. I told her we were going to the beach to wait for the sun to start setting.

Brannon

I insisted on going back to my cabin first, to change. I felt sweaty and, if I didn't get time to change before, I wanted to look better for my arrival in the Myst.

I put on one of my favourite dresses. It was black, with small white flowers as the print. The straps went over my shoulders, and it had a V-shaped neckline. The top half was fitted, and the bottom half flowed out a little. The back consisted of crisscrossed straps. My pendant was visible, glimmering on my chest. I put on the bracelet Asher got me for my birthday last year, with the symbol of our pendants put together, as a whole. I brushed out my hair, and it fell into bouncy waves. I had one last spritz of my favourite, floral perfume, with a hint of fruity essence, before leaving. The next time I returned to my bedroom it would be to enter my new life.

We turned the corner to the beach and that's when I saw everyone waiting. Mum and Marley. Tammy and Roger. Silvia and Blain. They were all standing, waving, and my heart burst.

"What's everyone doing here?" I asked Asher.

"Seeing you off," he said, rubbing my back with his hand.

Marley ran to me, struggling through the sand.

"Branny, you look beautiful," he said.

"Well, thank you. You look very handsome," I said, picking him up and pressing a kiss onto his cheek.

He was in a loose white shirt and beige chino shorts. He looked as though dad had dressed him as a mini version of himself.

I placed him back down and he walked beside me. We reached the group of adults, and his interest was diverted elsewhere, to the bucket and spade a few meters away.

"You guys didn't have to do this," I said.

"We wanted to," Tammy said. "You deserve it. And we wanted to say some things too.

"I know this won't be the last time I see you," Tammy continued, "but it feels like the perfect opportunity to thank you. You chose my son over everything. You're so brave and courageous and beautiful. It's been lovely watching you bring out the best in each other. I don't feel like I need to wish you luck on your next adventure, you'll be great."

She hugged me and my powers couldn't stop themselves from entering her mind and reading her emotions. She meant what she had said, but there was an underlying sense of worry that she hadn't mentioned. I guessed the worry wasn't for me, it was probably for Asher, and hoping that he'd be okay without me here all the time.

Roger stepped up next.

"I'm not good with words," he said, and we laughed at how true this was, "but I'll say this. If you were my daughter, proud wouldn't cut it."

He nodded his head at me and smiled. That was more than enough.

Silvia walked up to me, ready to say her part.

"I can't express how proud of you all I am. The three of you have saved the future of the Lunar witches." I saw a look of shock on my mum's face. Clearly, no one had warned Silvia to be filtered. "Brannon, I know you can leave, but I don't know how long I've got left. Just know that it was a pleasure watching you grow up and accept Blain for all he is. You are an amazing best friend, and an amazing person. I'll see you again, I'm sure. In the Myst."

I hugged her, not knowing how to thank her for her kindness.

"She's got a flare for drama," I heard Blain say to Tammy and Roger. I laughed under my breath.

I looked at Blain.

"I don't need to say goodbye, do I?" he said. "I'm coming with you."

"It wouldn't hurt to say something nice, though, would it Blain?" Silvia said, giving him a piercing stare.

He rolled his eyes then smiled at me. "I think you're the best person in this world," he said, "and you'll continue to be my best friend. It's not like I won't see you often. Asher needs the company and even said he'd fly me out here monthly!"

Asher

"I did not say that Blain," I said, laughing, and considering how his company might be a good thing.

Brannon looked at her mum, who looked like she was about to burst into tears. A tear spilled down her cheek.

"Sorry," she said, trying to smile. "I know you're not going forever but, as your mum, it's still hard."

"It's fine, mum," Brannon said, stroking her arm.

They looked into each other's eyes. A look of unconditional love between two lifelong friends, a mother and a daughter, who would always need each other. Forever.

"I'm so proud of you," Celia said, blabbing through the tears.

"I love you, mum."

"I love you, sweetie."

They hugged, then Celia waved her off.

"Go on," she said, "you better get going."

Brannon looked at the sky. The yellow sun was becoming orange and the sky was streaked with pink and purple. It was starting to set. Then, she looked at the floor, where Marley was playing.

"See you later, little man," she said, kneeling down to his level. "I've got to go now."

"Okay," he said, getting up and wrapping his tiny arms around her shoulders. "See you soon."

He went back to his sandcastle. Brannon smiled and stood back up.

"Right," she said, "let's go."

She stood between me and Blain as everyone hugged the three of us goodbye. Then we turned and walked down the beach.

I felt better knowing that everyone had a chance to say goodbye to Brannon. It wasn't really goodbye, but it felt like a farewell to life as we knew it.

We wasted no time getting into position when we got back. Brannon ran around her cabin, making sure everything was clean and in place. I assured her I'd keep it in pristine conditions, but I couldn't blame her for not believing me.

I suggested she lay down first. She swung her legs onto her bed and centred herself. She'd put three pillows out for us all, and her head rested softly on the middle one. She shut her eyes.

She didn't try to look as perfect as she did. It just came naturally to her. Her hair didn't look scruffy. It fell elegantly beside and behind her shoulders. Her eyelashes looked lengthy, although I already missed her lilac eyes. Her reddish lips were shut together gently. Her ankles were crossed, and her hands were intertwined, resting on her stomach. Her décolletage appeared smooth as I watched her chest move up and down slowly with every breath she took. It wasn't nearly as good as what I'd been used to, but I could get used to seeing her like this. A real-life sleeping beauty.

Blain and I lay on either side of her. Her bed was huge, so we fit with ease. Then we shut our eyes and joined her. In a place only the three of us now know.

Brannon

The goodbyes were over. It was time for the excitement to begin.

They joined me a few minutes later, and we all faced the sunset, melting into the horizon.

"How will Juno know it's time?" Blain asked. "It's always a sunset for her."

"She'll know we are here," I said. "She knows pretty much everything. She did create an entire afterlife."

"Good point," Blain said.

I loved being here with my best friend. I loved that he was finally a part of this. It felt right. We went through everything in life together, and I was glad this was now part of what we shared.

"Oh, look," Asher said, and our heads turned to the right, "There she is. But…wait…she's not alone."

"That's got to be Ancestor Selene," Blain said, sounding nervous all of a sudden. "Juno said she'd be here to do the spell, didn't she?"

"Yeah, you're right," Asher said.

"Guys, what do I do? How do I act?" Blain asked.

"What are you talking about?" I asked him.

"That's…like…my family," he said, shaking out his arms and hands.

"It's nothing," Asher said. "Be yourself."

Juno and Selene walked in sync, both in black cloaks, but with their hoods down. It was a purposeful power statement.

As they got closer, I noticed how Juno's eyes had come alive, now a vibrant violet in colour, matching her silver and purple hair. It was like looking at a wiser version of myself. She'd clearly put her necklace on.

My gaze turned to Selene. She was beautiful. She looked like she'd aged less than Juno, but a few decades more than us three. Her hair was thick and glistened like white snow under the sun. It was medium length and straight but flicked out at the very bottom. Her eyes were dark, mixed with a forest green, like Blain's. The coffee brown shade provided a pleasant contrast to her hair. If she was living in the Modern World, I could imagine she would have been chased by modelling agencies. Her sharp cheek bones and glowing skin indicated a youthful beauty to her that ageing clearly couldn't compete with.

She smiled at us. It was a kind smile.

Juno also had a kind smile, but it could easily translate as intimidating.

"Mr Curator, Mr Crescent and Miss Amory," Juno said, "it's my pleasure to introduce you to Ancestor Selene Crescent, leader of the Lunar witches."

Blain held his hand out. She looked at it, slightly thrown off, but shook it anyway.

"Hi," Blain said. "I'm Blain. Blain Crescent. My nan literally admires you."

Selene laughed, a grateful smile on her face. "How wonderful to hear," she said. "It's lovely to meet you, fellow Crescent."

Blain's grin was massive. I think he'd been waiting for this. For her approval.

"Nice to meet you," Asher said.

"And you, Mr Curator. Miss Amory," she turned to me, "it's a pleasure to meet you."

I smiled in reply.

"I believe a thank you is in order. I am grateful that you fought for the Lunar witches, after four centuries of us being forgotten. I am delighted to see the witches come together to correct histories mistakes. And I'm looking forward, Miss Amory, to seeing where the Myst takes you. I will be making an effort to stay in contact with you. After all, I would not be here without your perseverance and persistence, which I have heard much about."

Juno gave me a guilty shrug. It made me giggle.

"Let's get started, shall we?" Juno said, excitedly.

She instructed us to stand in a line in front of her. Blain would go first, then Asher, then me.

She approached Blain, placed her palm behind his necklace, and closed her eyes. She spoke words in what sounded like Latin to me. Her words lifted a breeze. I felt my hair move as the coolness travelled through it. Our surroundings looked like they'd been sprinkled with gold dust.

"Sigillum," she said.

I turned to look at Asher, widening my eyes and raising my eyebrows to silently ask him what she just said.

"She said 'seal'," he whispered. "She's sealing the magic in the necklace."

She closed her hand around the symbol of the crescent. When she released her grip again, the necklace looked like it had been restored to the shiniest silver. It glistened brilliantly on Blain's chest, a gleaming crescent.

"You represent the moon," she said.

Juno moved to Asher and did the same thing. When she released his pendant, we were all amazed to see that it was no longer a semi-circle. It was a full circle. A whole. Instead of rusted metal, it was solid gold.

"You represent the sun," she said.

She approached me, saying a few more Latin words than she had done with Blain and Asher. She removed her hand from my pendant, and I looked down immediately.

It was completely different. It looked like Blain's silver crescent symbol attached to half of Asher's golden sun.

"You represent all witches," she said.

She held eye contact with me and gave me a proud smile. One that said thank you, with no words needed.

"Perfect," she said. "They are all charged with the correct magic, prepared to perform their appropriate duties."

"Wonderful," Selene said.

I picked up my new pendant between my fingertips and analysed it. It was really happening. Four hundred years of continuity coming to an end.

Asher

The symbols reflected us perfectly. I thought the sun looked better gold, and the moon suited silver. Brannon got both, which made sense. The idea wasn't to mould the witches into one. There would always be two types. The Sol witches and the Lunar witches. This wasn't an attempt to change that. It was a movement to respect it.

"Now it's time for the ceremony," Juno said.

We stayed where we were, listening to Juno speak.

"Firstly, I thank you all. For sacrificing life as you know it to better the Myst. I appreciate that, in one aspect or another, the three of you have been thrown into the deep end of chaos, misunderstanding and the unknown. Each of you have embraced this rather than run from it, assuring me that the Myst could not be more fortunate than to have you all in its service.

"Mr Crescent, what a pleasure it has been to meet you. I grant you the title of leader of the Lunar witches. I have not known you for very long at all, but your heroic actions have proved enough. You have shown real courage and bravery. Everything your friends have said about you has proved to be true. I trust you'll make a phenomenal addition."

She turned to me, her purple eyes alive because she was wearing her own necklace, encapsulating her own power.

"Mr Curator, the leader of the Sol witches. It is my pleasure to grant you this title. If unrest occurs in the Myst, you will be summoned to settle and sort out the problems that your people have. Since knowing you, I have seen a considerate, understanding and incredibly loving young man. It is down to you that the Curator legacy proudly lives on."

She bowed her head to me. Juno's words meant a lot more to me than I could say. I knew if my dad heard this, he'd be proud.

"Miss Amory, the leader of all witches. From the moment I met you, I had a feeling you'd be far more than an anchor. Your wariness, inquisitiveness and ability to be headstrong stood out to be great qualities of a leader. In addition to this, you are sensitive, caring and, it is fair to say, you achieve what you desire. When I look at you, I am reminded of myself in youth. Not because you are all these great things, but because you see the potential of the supernatural world. Whilst I haven't always been sure you enjoy my presence, I have never had to question trusting you. You have proved that an Amory is not a bad person, simply because of the bloodline they were born into. It is my pleasure to stand with you, and my honour to view you as my partner."

Brannon's eyes welled up. There were no words to describe the look on her face. But I knew she'd been waiting for this. To be welcomed into the supernatural world with open, wanting arms.

"What a joyous ceremony. Such thoughtful words, Ancestor Juno," Selene said.

This experience reminded me of how much I hated the unknown. Uncertainty. I kept using my powers to see what the next couple of minutes would entail. I found it harder to do in the Myst. Things were blurred and I couldn't see a clear image.

I assumed too much was going on. My power wouldn't be able to compete with Juno's. Maybe she was unintentionally blocking my mind.

"It is now my honour to grant you a shared title.

"This journey began with the hope of uniting the witches. I feel it is appropriate to unite our three saviours under the same title.

"With that said, I shall make it official. The future of the Myst now falls into the palms of Mr Crescent, Mr Curator and Miss Amory…the Mysticals!"

We looked at each other, all beaming. The Mysticals. The perfect title. The perfect way to ensure that even when we wouldn't be together, we would be known as one.

Everything was coming together, just how it was meant to.

"Is it time for the spell?" Selene asked.

Juno nodded.

I tried to see the future, but I didn't have enough time. They had started to link hands, so I joined them.

Juno asked us all individually if we were ready to begin. We all said yes, so she closed her eyes and started to chant. Selene followed.

Brannon

The chanting was synchronised. I enjoyed listening to it, with my eyes shut, one hand in Asher's, one in Blain's.

"*Mystica mutatio aperta erit.*"

"The Myst will be open to change," Asher said, quietly informing Blain and me what was being said.

"*Luna plena surget et videbitur omni tempore.*"

Asher translated again, "A full moon will rise and be seen at all times."

"*Lunae potestas restituetur.*"

"Lunar power will be restored."

"*Aequas aditus potentiae habet strigae.*"

"The witches will have equal access to power."

"*Mutatio haec habita erit.*"

"This change will settle."

"*Caelum gratificari.*"

"The sky will oblige."

They repeatedly chanted the spell. The wind whipped through my hair. The ocean began to dance ferociously. The voices of Juno and Selene grew louder as the Myst unsettled.

We held each other's hands tighter. This was it. Everything was about to change.

Suddenly, the sun dropped. We were surrounded by nothing but darkness. I closed my eyes and squeezed their hands even tighter. The wind was howling, and the waves were violently crashing into the sand. Warmth disappeared and the cold breeze drew goosebumps out of my skin, all over my body.

Had something gone wrong? Was this meant to happen? Juno wasn't fighting for Selene's permission, so why had the sun fallen? I didn't understand. What did this mean?

But then everything stopped. The wind. The icy breeze. The waves. The chanting. I didn't open my eyes. I couldn't bear to see their disappointed faces as they told me the spell had failed.

"Oh my."

It was Asher. His alluring voice forced my eyes to open.

And that's when I saw it.

The sky was violet. It faded into an amethyst, then into a burnt orange as it met with the sea. It looked surreal. Like nothing I'd seen before. It was supernatural.

I noticed a strip of light through the water.

There was a glow shining brightly behind a silver ball. The whole sky had changed. And, for the first time, I saw what it looked like. When the sun collided with the moon.

"What just happened?" Blain asked, his voice quiet with wonder.

Everyone was staring up at it, eyes completely glued to the sky. The spell worked. The Myst changed.

Juno spoke, eyes full of wisdom, and a voice loaded with astonishment, "It's a total eclipse of the witches."

Asher

It was as if we had journeyed to another planet. I had never seen a sky blend from such a neon purple to a vibrant but rusted orange. The glow from the sun was still blinding as it stood proudly above the ocean, but the middle of it was now masked by the moon.

Whilst it was a sight I couldn't wait to see when I was next brought here, it meant that it was finished. The wait was over.

"What an incredible sight," Selene said, staring in awe.

"It really is," Juno said. "Congratulations, the Myst has been restored with lunar power."

"I don't understand," Blain said, mesmerised by the view above.

"It is simple, really. The sky is reflecting the power of the Myst. Before, it was solar, with a lingering sense of potential for lunar. However, the uniting of the witches has changed that, because the power is now equally solar and lunar," Selene explained.

Silence fell as our gaze returned to the sky. It was a sight you wouldn't get sick of. Couldn't.

It was a few minutes before I decided to speak. "What happens now?"

Brannon looked worried. We knew what happened next. She knew how much I didn't want to face it.

"Mr Curator, I am pleased to announce the success of the spell. Soon, Miss Amory and I must go. We must explain to the community of the Myst what has happened. I am positive there will be chaos erupting as we speak," Juno said.

"Sounds like you'll have your hands full," I said, directing it to Brannon, trying to take her mind off me. I didn't want her to worry about how I'd be feeling. I wanted her to enjoy what awaited her.

"Are you going now?" Blain asked, trying to figure out whether he should hug Brannon one last time.

"In a moment, yes," Juno said. "There is one last thing."

"What is it?" Brannon asked.

"Mr Curator, Mr Crescent, whilst we will be eternally grateful for the roles you both play now, I think you will agree that without Miss Amory none of this would have happened." Juno faced Brannon, holding her hands in her own. "Miss Amory, you have fixed a problem that I should've fixed many, many moons ago. A mistake I should have erased before your first sunset. I know you would not expect anything, but I wanted desperately to thank you.

"I could only think of one thing that would truly show my appreciation for you. So, I occupied every second of my spare time figuring out how I could do that. And I am happy to report, I was successful."

I used every ounce of power I could to push my mind into the future. Suddenly my vision wasn't blurry anymore. I could see everything. Clearly.

"Miss Amory, I think you'll be pleased to know that your father is no longer suffering. I transferred the power that was disabling his body into your new pendant."

And then the future I saw became the present.

Brannon

Asher gasped, quickly moving his hand over his mouth.

I took a step away from Juno, to see what he'd seen in the distance.

Suddenly, the sky looked brighter, and the sun felt warmer. In seconds, my body was covered in goosebumps.

I saw someone walking towards me. A man. He had dusty grey hair. Silver, really. He wasn't old. He was able. Late forties. He was wearing brown, lace up shoes. Not trainers, proper shoes. Beige shorts and a white shirt. The type of outfit you'd wear to the beach. Convenient for a stroll…under the starlight.

And then it hit me. Like a sunbeam in the eye.

"Dad?"

Asher

The word escaped her mouth in a whisper. Tears spilled down her face.

She took a few slow steps past us. Gradually, her walk became a run. And then a sprint. Nothing could stop her. Nothing.

Her foot hit the ground one last time before she pushed her weight off and jumped into his arms. I could hear her crying. He picked her up and swung her round.

Brannon

He smelt of home. That was all.
He held my face in his hands.
I was home. I was safe.
"There's my girl. My beautiful Brannon."
His voice.
"Why are you here, dad?" I sobbed.
His thumbs wiped away my tears.
"I've come to walk you through the sun."
The sun.
He was the sun.

Asher

Nothing else mattered now. It didn't have to. I didn't care that I was going home alone. This. This is how it should be. This is what mattered.

"Without the power in his body, he can live like the rest of us in the Myst," Juno said, wiping a tear from her own cheek.

"You are simply incredible, Juno," Selene said.

"You really are," I said.

I looked at Blain. Tears were streaming down his cheeks. I put an arm around his shoulders as we watched the Amory's walk to us.

"Miss Amory, I hope this shows you how grateful I am," Juno said.

Brannon nodded her head, unable to talk.

Mr Amory held his hand out to me. "Thank you," he said, "for looking after her."

I shook his hand. He cupped it with his other.

It was good to see him again.

Brannon

Blain walked up to him and hugged him.

"Inseparable, as always," he said, rolling his eyes at me and Blain.

We laughed. We always laughed with dad.

"That is all," Juno said. "We may leave now."

I couldn't believe it. I couldn't explain how I felt. It was indescribable. But I had no doubts, now. This is where I was meant to be.

"Let's give them a moment," Juno said, "for there will never be enough."

She wanted to let me and Asher say goodbye. He would return to his life at camp. I would explore my new life in the Myst, with my dad.

"Will you two do me a favour?" my dad asked Blain and Asher. "Tell Celia I love her. And tell Marley to keep making me proud."

They nodded.

Juno, Selene, Blain and my dad left us to ourselves.

I turned to face Asher. He was looking at me like I was the best thing in his world.

"So," I said, not knowing how to do this.

"So," he said back.

"He's here, Asher. My dad," I said.

"I know, gorgeous."

"I get to do this with him."

"It will be amazing," Asher said.

"And I'll see you soon. To tell you all about it," I said.

"I know you will."

He stroked his thumb over my cheek.

"You really are the best thing in my world," he said.

I smiled and turned my head to kiss the palm of his hand.

"It's not goodbye, remember?" I said.

He kissed my lips. A kiss full of want and passion. And most importantly, full of love.

"Now go," he said, "the Myst awaits you."

A single tear escaped his ocean blue eyes and fell down his cheek. I wiped it away.

"I love you," I said.

"I love you," he replied.

"To the moon and never back?" I asked, smiling.

"To the moon and never back," he said, smiling too.

We walked to join the others.

I gave Blain another hug. Then we left. Headed for the Myst.

I tried not to look back. Not out of fear that I'd change my mind about this. But because I didn't want to see them cry.

Dad wrapped an arm around my shoulders and said what I needed to hear. Dads are good at that. Knowing what you need to hear.

"My beautiful Brannon. I know it's true, because it's happened twice now," he said, as we walked through the water. "My life starts when yours does."

Asher

Mr Amory's return was a miracle. A blessing.

I didn't find myself worrying about Brannon. I didn't have to question her safety. I knew she was okay. She was with him. Her dad.

I spent every day thinking about her. It didn't matter how much energy I put into work and camp; my thoughts always went back to Brannon. Wondering when I'd see her next.

They say distance makes the heart grow fonder, and it definitely does.

Even when she wasn't by my side, filling my life with laughter and my heart with love, I felt her presence. Everywhere.

I often found myself sitting on the pier, dangling my legs above the water and sharing my feelings with the ocean. It was our favourite place when she was here, and my favourite place whilst she's gone. I could feel her here. Beside me. Listening.

I made an effort not to forget what she'd taught me. She'd taught me to care for others. To live for every moment. To love recklessly. And relentlessly. And blindly.

From the moment I met her, I knew she was important. More than important. She changed me. She completed me.

I thought about her constantly. How happy she'd be right now. Finally living a life she was happy with.

That's what love is. Wanting someone else to be happy.

She didn't have to be here for me to appreciate her. She was every word. Every breath. Everything.

And every day, as I watch the sun set, I'll fall in love with her all over again. Always.

Forever.

Brannon

I had hoped for something extraordinary.
    And truthfully?
    It was more than that.

The End

The Myst Saga

he was the sun
to the moon and never back
total eclipse of the witches

Lauren Vinn

Acknowledgements

And the sun sets on the Myst Saga…

Thank you to everyone who has shown support to me and my first three books. I owe the biggest thank you to the readers, who have journeyed through the Myst with me. When I first penned '*he was the sun*' I had no idea that it would soon become a published trilogy.

Ian Hooper at Leschenault Press, thank you for everything you've done. I have learnt so much from you, and feel very grateful to have received your invaluable advice.

I owe a special thank you to my amazing family, for your unconditional support in everything I do. I'm going to use this opportunity to truly thank you all, because I wouldn't be where I am without you.

Dad (the three peaks, coast to coast, 8x tough mudder, rat race legend), you taught me that life isn't all sunshine and rainbows, and this is advice that I will always carry with me. However, I've found that on my walk through life with you, there's never a lack of sunshine, and behind every cloud is a rainbow. I wouldn't be able to write about the extraordinary love between a father and daughter without knowing how it feels for myself. Thank you for being my wingman.

My mum, the real life superwoman. You're the most hardworking childminder, the most caring friend and the most inspiring mother. Your love for us never sets with the sun, it keeps us warm under every moon. The woman I am today, and the one I hope to be, I owe to you. Thank you for being my best friend.

Jamie, I'm sure you'll probably never pick this book up to read it, which means you'll probably never see this, but I guess I can't leave you out. Even though you're considerably taller than me, having a little brother like you has been a blessing. With you till the end of the line, always.

Lacey, my reflection and opposition. Thank you for being my biggest supporter, and one of the funniest people in my life. I won't always have the answers to your problems, but you'll never have to face them alone. I promise on our sister friendship, forever.

Nanny Jean and Nanny Jill, thank you for showing me strength. Grandad Tony, thank you for making me laugh. And finally, Grandad Chris. Thank you for showing me the way to writing.

I love you all. More than that.

Lauren
Cambridgeshire
2022

About the Author

Lauren Vinn was born in London, and now lives in Cambridgeshire. She is currently studying English Literature and Writing at Cambridgeshire's Ruskin University.

During the first lockdown of 2020, Lauren explored her passion of writing by penning this, her first novella, '*he was the sun*'. Whilst growing up, writing was, and still is, her favourite thing to do. She believes that words are the most invaluable source of power, and that mum is always right…Always.

When she is not writing, she is reading. Or, although aware that this is nothing to be proud of, watching the same few movies and television series on repeat.

Above all, something that Lauren enjoys more than anything is surrounding herself with family and friends. She believes that writing, reading and spending time with her loved ones are the things that keep her happy. However, if all else fails, she finds a sunset. This, in Lauren's eyes, has never failed.

To keep in contact, visit: @LVwritingx